The world is in peril.

A long-forgotten evil has risen from the far corners of Erdas, and we need YOU to help stop it.

Claim your spirit animal and join the adventure now:

1. Go to scholastic.com/spiritanimals.

2. Log in to create your character and choose your own spirit animal.

3. Have your book ready and enter the code below to unlock the adventure.

Your code:

N462WJF4WM

By the Four Fallen,
The Greencloaks

It shimmered under the dark sky, glowing as if from within, a rainbow of silver and gold.

The Evertree.

THE EVERTREE

Marie Lu

SCHOLASTIC INC.

To Taylor, who loves
beasts great and small
—M.L.

❖

Library of Congress Control Number: 2014957423

ISBN 978-0-545-59977-1
10 9 8 7 6 5 4 3 2 1   15 16 17 18 19

Book design by Charice Silverman
Map illustration by Michael Walton

Library edition, April 2015

Printed in the U.S.A.   23

Scholastic US: 557 Broadway • New York, NY 10012
Scholastic Canada: 604 King Street West • Toronto, ON • M5V 1E1
Scholastic New Zealand Limited: Private Bag 94407 • Greenmount, Manukau 2141
Scholastic UK Ltd.: Euston House • 24 Eversholt Street • London NW1 1DB

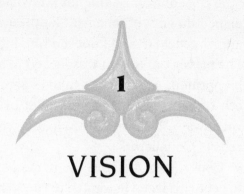

VISION

Enormous black scales slithering across grass. A gorilla's earthshaking roar. A piercing shriek from the sky. Grass, dirt, rock, brittle bark. A heartbeat deep in the earth, something as old as time itself. A silhouette of twisting antlers that appeared and then vanished.

The dream always began this way. Conor blinked, blinded by the light overhead. He held his hand out over his eyes in an attempt to block it, but the light cut through, turning the edges of his skin red and translucent. Something gold flashed before his eyes. It vanished immediately, but for that instant, it had looked like leaves. He struggled to a sitting position. The dirt beneath him crumbled, hard and cracked, dying.

A voice echoed in the air.

Conor. It is the end of an era. We need you here.

Tellun? Conor thought. Gradually, he realized that the blinding light came from fires. Fire was everywhere.

"Conor!"

Conor jerked his head to his side at the familiar scream. As his eyes adjusted to the light, he realized that he was lying near the edge of a cliff – and not far from him stood Meilin, weighed down with chains. She threw herself at an oncoming Greencloak and knocked him into the dirt. Jhi looked helplessly on. Rollan was locked in a tight battle with an enormous snake. The snake wrapped its coils around both of his arms, lifting him high in the air. A short distance away, Abeke and Uraza fought what seemed like hundreds of Conquerors.

Briggan! Conor tried to shout the name as he finally managed to get to his feet. He wanted to run to his friends. Why was it so hard to move? *Briggan, come on! We have to help them – where are you?* He called and called for his wolf before he realized that Briggan was in his passive state. But something seemed wrong. The longer Conor stared at the tattoo, the fainter it turned, until he couldn't tell whether or not it was there at all. His heart seized in terror.

Conor.

The gorilla's roar sounded out again, shaking the earth beneath his feet. Conor looked off to a large rock behind where Rollan struggled with the snake. There stood the Great Ape. One of his fists pounded heavily against his chest, while the other fist clutched what looked like a twisted golden staff that gave off a strange, ethereal glow.

The ape swiveled his head toward Conor in such an eerie move that it sent shivers down his spine. The shadow that the beast cast swallowed Conor whole, covering every bit of land as far as the eye could see. When the ape caught sight of Conor, he narrowed his eyes into dangerous slits. Then he threw his head back into another roar. He charged him.

Run! Conor screamed at himself, but his limbs all felt like they were dragging through thick molasses. He tried to lunge forward with each step, only to feel like he was being pulled back. Behind him, the gorilla surged forward, his mighty limbs pounding against the earth. Conor ran toward the edge of the cliff, unsure what he expected to do once he got there. He skidded to a halt just over the edge, arms wheeling. His boots kicked up a shower of pebbles that rained over the cliff side. There was nowhere else to go.

The gorilla roared behind him. He was so close now. Conor cowered near the cliff's edge. All he could see around him were the images of his friends losing the war, struggling against enemies far too strong for them. Greencloaks fell before Conquerors and flames rose into the sky, all against the backdrop of a bleak, dying land.

The gorilla reached him. Conor's boot slipped. He tried to catch himself, but all he caught was a close glimpse of the gorilla's terrifying eyes. He teetered on the edge.

An enormous eagle appeared overhead. Its wings gleamed bronze and white as they blocked out the sun. Conor looked up at it, and to his amazement, he saw Tarik riding on its back, his cloak billowing out behind him. *Tarik! You're alive!* An indescribable joy and relief washed over him at the sight of the familiar face. Tarik was here. Everything was going to be okay. The Greencloak reached out with one gloved hand toward Conor, and Conor reached up to take it.

Except it wasn't Tarik.

The face transformed. The kind, knowing eyes were replaced with ones cold and cunning. Conor found himself staring up into the face of Shane instead. The boy smiled at him in a way that showed all his teeth at once. In the distance, the gorilla's roar mixed with Tellun's deep voice. Shane withdrew his hand, and Conor saw the abyss yawn beneath him, swallowing him whole.

2

SLEEPWALKING

I T WAS A COLD, DRIZZLY MORNING AT GREENHAVEN CASTLE. Rollan wrapped his cloak – *Tarik's* old green cloak, rather – more tightly around his shoulders and wandered out to the main entrance, where he'd seen Abeke surveying the overcast landscape with Uraza at her side. The Coral Octopus hung heavily around his neck, bumping against his chest with every step he took. He found himself reaching up frequently to touch it. After all that had happened – Shane's betrayal, Meilin's turning, Tarik's death – he couldn't afford to lose one of their two remaining talismans.

How long had it been since Shane escaped with the talismans? A few weeks? Somehow, the whole thing felt like it'd happened yesterday. And here they were, still gathering Greencloaks from around the world, building up their forces to face the Conquerors. Rollan's mouth tightened in frustration. If Tarik were here, he would tell Rollan not to worry, to calm down and think clearly, to let himself grieve and then move forward with a clear, patient head. But all Rollan could do these days was pace restlessly in the castle, waiting for the word that they could head out to retrieve the talismans, stop Kovo the Ape, and rescue Meilin.

And rescue Meilin.

His fingers stopped fiddling with the Coral Octopus for a moment, suspended by the weight of the thought. Rescuing her felt impossible. Sometimes, when he chatted with the others, he found himself looking for Meilin so that he could tell her the newest joke in his head. He would yearn to make her laugh, only to realize that she wasn't there. She was far away.

Rollan sighed. He couldn't afford to keep thinking about all that had gone wrong. He closed his eyes, took a deep breath, and tried to pretend that Tarik was still wandering around somewhere in the castle, that Meilin was asleep in her chambers upstairs. He knew neither was true, but right now, he could force himself to believe, and it kept his darker thoughts at bay.

The weather. That was a much safer thought. *I'll think about the weather.*

For the fifteenth time that morning, Rollan considered how odd the weather had been. This was supposed to be the dry season, but for the past week, as Olvan organized their forces in preparation to leave, they'd gotten nothing but gray skies and steady rain. Even the animals were behaving oddly all of a sudden. The birds were migrating early, for one, and when Rollan looked overhead, he could see another flock heading south in two giant V formations.

"Go ahead, Essix," he murmured to his gyrfalcon, who sat perched on his shoulder. If she kept putting her full weight on him like this, he was going to get a sore back for sure. "I know you want to hunt."

But even Essix seemed out of sorts. She chirped a little, fluffed her neck feathers to shake out water droplets, and settled in even more. She seemed completely content to stay put, instead of heading out for a good hunt. Rollan watched her for a while. When she just went back to preening her tail feathers, he tried to ignore his aching shoulder and decided he'd better leave her be. Far be it from him to judge her sullen mood.

Maybe she loathed waiting around just as much as Rollan did.

By the time he reached the castle entrance, the drizzle had turned into a steady rain. The water beaded on the fabric of his cloak before soaking through. Uraza watched them approach. Her tail swished back and forth. Even though she wasn't his spirit animal, Rollan guessed she probably felt a little impatient with all the waiting too.

Abeke stood beside her, leaning against the archway and absently stroking the leopard's velvety head. She didn't bother turning when Rollan came to join her. The Granite Ram, their only other talisman, dangled from her neck, the pale gray pendant prominent against the dark of her skin.

"Hey," Rollan said. "I know you were supposed to be your village's Rain Dancer and all, but can you lighten up on all the dancing?" He looked up at the sky for emphasis.

Abeke's eyes flickered to Rollan's cloak, then went back to surveying the bleak landscape. She didn't seem amused by his joke, and in embarrassment, he let it fade away. "Hey," she just said.

Rollan turned serious. "Olvan says we should be able to set out soon, in the next few days."

"Any new messages?"

He shook his head. They'd sent out dozens of stormy petrels and pigeons to their Greencloak allies and friends in other nations, hoping that some of them would receive the call for help in time to come to their aid. Abeke had sent several doves to Nilo, to deliver the news to her father and sister.

Friends — we make for Stetriol in a week. We need your help.

As far as Rollan knew, Abeke's father hadn't responded.

"Sorry," he replied.

Abeke nodded her thanks, lowered her eyes, and turned away again.

Rollan pursed his lips, for once lacking a witty quip. Where was a good joke when you needed one? Abeke had been like this often lately, staring off at the horizon while lost in thought. He knew she was probably dwelling on Shane's betrayal, and how Meilin had been forced to turn on all of them. And by the way she lowered her eyes in shame, he knew she still blamed herself for all of it.

Meilin. Again, Rollan scolded himself for returning to the thoughts that kept him tossing at night and pushing away his meals. *Where is she now?* he wondered. What was she thinking?

What must it feel like, to have no power over yourself?

The pain of losing Meilin irritated him for an instant. He'd done so well, for so long, on his own. But now there were people at stake, whose absences hurt him, and he didn't like it one bit.

As if she could tell what he was thinking, Abeke tilted her head toward him and cleared her throat. "It looks good on you," she said, offering him a weak smile.

Tarik's cloak. Memories flashed back to him of the elder Greencloak's last stand, of the hopeful look in Tarik's eyes when he saw his own cloak draped in Rollan's arms, just before he sacrificed himself. A pain spread in Rollan's chest, until he felt like he could barely breathe.

Still, there was something comforting about Abeke's words. As if Tarik wasn't completely gone. Even now, the cloak protected him, shielding him from the rain. Essix ruffled her feathers again, and flecks of water went flying.

"Thanks," he muttered. "Who knew I'd have to wrap myself up to keep warm at this time of year?"

"Olvan says the Greencloaks in Nilo are reporting weird weather there too."

"Like what?"

"Like layers of ice over the watering holes. He said some of the animals don't know what to make of it, and they can't get to the water."

Ice. In Nilo? Rollan tried to imagine the oasis where they'd found Cabaro, encased in a thick layer of ice. "Well. *That* sounds like a nice, normal summer."

Abeke couldn't help smiling a little at his sarcasm. "I can't remember seeing that — or even hearing about it — when I lived in Nilo. The tribes must be in chaos."

"Or skating around and playing games. I mean, *I* would."

That coaxed a genuine laugh out of her. "I can see it. Planks of wood and antelope bone strapped to our feet."

Rollan leaned in with a conspiratorial grin. "I bet Uraza

would love that. Wouldn't you?" He nodded at Uraza, who regarded him with a rather withering look.

The two chuckled a little, and then their moment of humor faded.

Rollan realized that Abeke must be wondering how her father and sister were doing. He shifted his boots against the damp stone floor. "Do you think they're okay?" he asked.

Abeke shrugged. For a moment, she threw her shoulders back in an illusion of confidence. "I haven't thought much about it," she said, almost too careful about her carelessness.

The lie in her words and posture was so obvious that Rollan could have sensed it even without his gifts from Essix. Still, he just nodded along. He had lost his mentor, the only man he'd ever thought of as a father . . . but Abeke's *true* father had turned his back on her. And the person Abeke had always considered a good friend — Shane — had used her friendship too.

"Abeke," Rollan suddenly said, touching her arm with his hand. She and Uraza both turned to look at him in unison. "Look. I know what you must be going through. You don't have to pretend around me." He hesitated. He'd never been all that good at gestures of serious emotion. "It's not your fault," he finally said. "Shane's betrayal . . . He's the one who should feel guilty, not you. You couldn't have known. You love and you trust. And I just wanted to say . . . well, that I'm sorry people keep taking advantage of that trust."

Abeke studied him for a long moment. She still looked sad, but Rollan thought he could see some of the guilt lift from her eyes. After a while, she nodded. "Thank you," she murmured. "I'm sorry that you've had to wait so long to trust others," she replied.

The two fell into a comfortable silence. After a while, Rollan shook his head and nudged her gently. "The ice will pass, I know it. All I can say is that I'd be mad if Nilo was hogging all the blue sky and sunshine."

Abeke cracked a wry smile. Uraza let out a comforting rumble deep in her throat, then nudged the girl's hand with her head.

Suddenly Rollan felt Essix's weight shift on his shoulder. An instant later, she pushed off from him and launched herself into the air with an earsplitting shriek. The movement nearly sent him tumbling backward. He flinched, his ears ringing, and looked on as she soared up into the sky. "Hey!" he shouted up at her, annoyed. "I know you're loud – you don't have to show off!"

"What is she doing?" asked Abeke.

"I don't know. Probably decided she was hungry after all." But the migrating birds were too far off in the distance now. Something else must have caught her attention. Rollan looked at Essix as she flew farther away –

– and then, abruptly, the world rushed forward around him, and he could see through her eyes.

He soared up, up, above the castle and into the open air, and then he looked down at where their small figures stood at the entrance. Essix's gaze turned sharply to focus on one of the castle's battlements. She shrieked again. This time, it was the distinct cry of something going very, very wrong.

Rollan looked closer. There, along the slippery, wet edge of the battlement's stone barrier, walked *Conor*.

Conor didn't walk in a concentrated way. He swayed and teetered dangerously along the ledge, as if he wasn't quite awake. The hairs rose on the back of Rollan's neck. *What on Erdas is he doing up there?* Rollan blinked, feeling his vision rush back to the ground and return to him. He pointed up in horror.

"Is that *Conor*?" he said incredulously.

"What?" Abeke exclaimed. She looked too. Immediately she straightened, then squinted as if she couldn't quite believe what she was seeing either. She cupped her hands around her mouth. *"Conor!"* she shouted up at the battlement. "Hey, *Conor!*"

But Conor didn't seem to hear her. He didn't seem to notice anything, actually, not even the fact that he was now inching his way along the edge of the battlement. Where was Briggan? Rollan glanced frantically around the top of the tower, but the enormous gray wolf was nowhere to be seen. Briggan must have been in his passive state.

A chill ran down Rollan's spine as he thought back to Meilin's strange, Bile-addled behavior. *What if Conor was somehow affected by the Bile too?* Rollan felt a sudden urge to call out for Tarik—until he remembered, with a pang, that Tarik was no longer there to help them.

"Come on!" he hissed at Abeke, grabbing her hand. He dashed through the entrance, back into the castle, and toward the stairs leading up to the battlement. They ran up the steps two at a time. Rollan almost tripped on one step, but caught himself and hurried on. Uraza bounded beside them, each of her strides equal to three of theirs.

By the time they emerged at the top of the wet battlement, Uraza was already there. Rollan wiped rain out of his eyes, and his gaze settled on Conor's teetering figure.

No!

Essix shrieked again and dove for the boy. Rollan lunged forward as fast as he could.

He reached Conor—right as Conor slipped off the edge.

THE PLAN

Essix dove at the same time Rollan cried out. Her talon hooked into the sleeve of Conor's shirt. The fabric ripped — but not all the way. For an instant, Conor dangled precariously in midair.

"Grab him!" Rollan shouted.

Abeke was the closest. She skidded to a crouch on the ledge, using one hand to securely grasp the stone battlement. Then she stretched her free arm out to grab Conor's sleeve. Essix flapped as close as she could — but with each movement, the fabric tore more, until nothing but a few dozen threads kept Conor from plummeting to the ground.

Abeke finally seized Conor's sleeve. She tightened her fist around it and pulled him toward her. The boy groaned at the movement. His eyes opened for the first time — initially, he looked disoriented. Then he glanced down and gasped.

The threads of the fabric snapped.

Conor fell. Abeke gritted her teeth and hung on tight. Conor slammed into the side of the wall, grunting in pain. Abeke hung desperately on to his sleeve, but she could feel her grip slipping. Just when she thought she could hold on no longer, Uraza stretched her neck out and seized Conor's arm in her mouth. She tugged, careful not to break Conor's skin with her teeth.

"Pull!" Abeke shouted, working as one with Uraza. Conor looked up at her and used his other hand to grab her wrist. She clenched her jaw. Then Rollan joined her in pulling Conor up, and together they dragged him back over the side of the tower.

The three collapsed in a heap, right as two Greencloaks came running.

"What's all this?" It was Olvan, and his eyebrows were furrowed.

Abeke stayed where she sat, still trying to catch her breath. Beside her, Uraza blinked water out of her violet eyes and swished her tail. She seemed agitated, enough so that she actually growled at the Greencloaks whenever they got too close to her.

"You tell *us*," Abeke finally said to Conor, who looked unsure of what had just happened himself. The side of his cheek that had slammed into the tower was already beginning to bruise.

Rollan leaned back and rubbed his shoulder. "Yeah, what was that all about? Recreational attempt at flying? If you wanted to do that, you should've let Essix know ahead of time."

Olvan turned his piercing eyes to Conor. "You were climbing the battlement, boy?"

Conor didn't say a word. Abeke watched him carefully as he pulled himself into a sitting position and wiped the rain from his face. He seemed deep in thought. She couldn't guess what he was possibly thinking about, aside from having just narrowly escaped death. It took her a moment to *see* everything wrong with him—he looked particularly pale, and whether his hair was plastered to his face from rain or sweat, she couldn't tell. Dark circles rimmed the bottom of his eyes.

Olvan helped him to his feet, threw his own cloak around Conor's shoulders, and guided him away from the battlement. He motioned for Abeke and Rollan to follow. "Let's get you three out of the rain. This is no way to start a morning."

An hour later, Abeke, Rollan, and Conor were sitting in the dining hall in fresh, dry clothes, all wrapped in blankets and sipping hot porridge. Abeke's braids were still plastered to her scalp, matted down with rain. Steam rose from their heads. She sipped her breakfast gratefully, thinking that if only the porridge had a touch of Niloan spice in it, it could be the best thing she'd ever eaten in her life. Nearby, Rollan was gulping his own porridge down, not even bothering with a spoon. It was the first time this week that Abeke had seen him with an appetite.

Olvan and Lenori sat nearby, as if they feared something else might happen if they left Conor alone. Conor just stirred his bowl of porridge. His eyes focused on nothing in particular, and Abeke thought she could hear him muttering under his breath. Briggan sat beside him with his muzzle in Conor's lap. Conor stroked his head absently.

Abeke finally decided to break the silence. She nudged Conor. "So . . . what happened up there?" she asked him carefully. "Sleepwalking?" She didn't want to accuse him aloud of what she knew they all feared — that Meilin had sleepwalked too, when Gerathon controlled her through the Bile. But Conor seemed to hear the concern in her voice.

"It's not that," he said, hesitating. "At least, I don't think so." Conor stayed silent for a moment longer. Then he put his spoon down and nodded. "I've been having dreams again . . . ever since Shane took the talismans." Rollan sucked in his breath sharply, but Conor went on. "I'm okay, but I haven't slept well, and I keep dreaming the same things night after night." He hesitated. "I woke up in the middle of the night last week too . . . and found myself climbing the battlement."

A chill ran down Abeke's spine. She didn't want to think about what might have happened if Conor hadn't woken himself up in time, and if no one had been around to help him.

Rollan raised an eyebrow. "You could've, you know, *told* someone. I would have happily stood outside your door and whacked you in the head every time you tried to leave."

"Rollan has a valid point," Olvan agreed. "Why did you leave Briggan in his passive state after your first incident, and tell none of your friends?"

Conor shrugged, looking guilty. "I would have, except I had a night when nothing happened. So I thought it went away. I even locked my bedroom door — but I must have unlocked it in my sleep."

Lenori leaned forward, the beads around her neck clacking together. Her eyes were warm with concern. "What dreams did you have, Conor?" she said gently. "Do you remember?"

Conor took a deep breath. "They started a few weeks ago." He frowned. "There's always an ape. And the shadow of antlers. A bright flash of light. Golden leaves." Conor looked out the window, his expression distant as he relived the vision. "We are all in the middle of a battle. The ape attacks me. I fall over a cliff, but a man riding an eagle soars overhead. At first, I think it's Tarik coming to my rescue." Rollan stiffened at the late Greencloak's name. "But when I reach out to take his hand, I see that it isn't Tarik at all. It's Sha—"

Conor cut himself off, but Abeke still winced. She knew the name hanging on the tip of his tongue. She knew it all too well.

Conor cleared his throat. "Anyway, he pretends to save me, and then he lets me fall," he finished, shooting Abeke a sympathetic look.

Abeke tightened her jaw and tried to push Shane from her mind, but it was hard not to imagine his face. Hard not to imagine how Shane had looked when he rode away on Halawir's back with the talismans. And now Conor was having dreams about it.

How earnest and sincere Shane had seemed, when he sailed to Greenhaven with her and convinced her to vouch for him, when he'd asked for her help and lied through his teeth without a single flicker of his gaze. How silly she had been, to believe him. *I love that you have that much faith about people. You really are amazing.*

The words echoed, familiar and cruel, in her ears. How *stupid.*

"Abeke." Conor's voice jerked her out of the memory.

"Huh?" she blurted out.

Rollan was staring at her too, with a concerned look on his face. "We said, are you okay?"

Abeke shook her head, blinked, and straightened. Her mouth set back into a line. "I'm fine," she replied. "Conor, what do you think your dreams mean? Are they prophetic? I thought you couldn't do that if Briggan was in his passive state, and you said—"

"I know," Conor agreed. "That's what I thought too. But it keeps happening, night after night. I don't know what's causing them, but I know they mean something."

"What do they mean, then?" Rollan said.

Conor took a deep breath. His eyes darted to Olvan before settling back on his friends. "Kovo has stirred in his prison. I think Shane and Zerif have reached him, or are going to reach him soon. We're going to fight a great war in Stetriol."

The hall fell silent at Conor's ominous words. After a moment, he went on. "I don't know what the golden leaves mean, but . . . every time I saw them, I felt a heartbeat under my feet, something deep and powerful in the ground."

"The heart of the lands," Lenori murmured in wonder, and everyone turned to her. She nodded at Conor. "There is an ancient myth among the Amayan tribes of a place in Erdas that is the origin of all life—humans, animals, even the Great Beasts. The tale calls this the place where the heart of our world still beats. Perhaps what you felt was the birthplace of Erdas. If so, there is a lot more at stake than we thought."

Abeke's heart skipped a beat. She had heard similar myths as a little girl, tales that named Nilo as the first of the lands.

Rollan cleared his throat. "Did you see anything about Meilin?" he asked, the hope obvious in his voice.

Conor met the other boy's eyes reluctantly. "I saw her and Jhi fighting Greencloaks, with the Conquerors at her back. They disappeared into the fray."

Rollan's entire posture drooped. His face darkened as he returned to his porridge. Abeke could tell that Conor regretted saying anything at all.

Olvan sat taller in his seat and gave the three as comforting of a look as he could. "These are visions, not yet truth," he reminded them. "All is not yet lost. And we received several new messages this morning."

At that, Abeke leaned forward. "From whom? Where?"

"Our friends Finn, Kalani, and Maya will arrive in Greenhaven tomorrow."

Maya! Kalani! It would be good to see them again. Finn too. Abeke waited for him to list a few more names, but the elder Greencloak finished, and the hall settled back into an uneasy silence. Her face fell again. Her father's name was not among them. Why was she surprised? Still, she managed a smile. "No others?" she asked hopefully.

Olvan shook his head, clearly dismayed that he could not give her better news. "With Conor's prophecy, we cannot wait any longer. We will take two parties and set out separately." He looked at the others. "Abeke, Rollan, and Conor—you will travel with a small patrol of our best Greencloaks. You will move faster and more stealthily this way, giving you the chance to search for Kovo's prison and the stolen talismans. I will lead a larger force of Greencloaks from a different direction and meet you there. Too many Conquerors will be gathered in Stetriol for your smaller team to face alone – our forces will provide a distraction for the Conquerors, so that you are able to get through and carry out your mission."

A brief silence fell over them. Abeke saw Rollan's eyes wander over to the empty chair beside Lenori. Tarik would have sat there. He would have been at this meeting, and his presence would have reassured them. Now there was only an echo of him in the air, a ghost. Abeke knew Rollan must be thinking about that now. He pushed his porridge bowl away, as if suddenly uninterested.

"What about Tellun?" Rollan muttered. He looked around. "I mean, there's still the Platinum Elk."

Lenori shook her head. "I have not seen nor felt Tellun's presence."

Olvan folded his hands before him. "We cannot afford a separate mission to find Tellun and the Platinum Elk. There is no time to lose."

"Conor said he saw a shadow of antlers in his dream," Abeke added. "Maybe that's where we'll find Tellun too, at the heart of Erdas."

Rollan nodded, probably relieved that they could finally be on the move again. If they had to wait any longer to go after Shane and rescue Meilin . . .

Conor still had a troubled look on his face. Abeke reached out and tapped his arm. "What's the matter?" she said, a knot of dread tightening in her stomach. "Is there more to what you saw?"

Conor nodded. This time, his stare focused not on his friends, but on their spirit animals. He met Essix's piercing eyes, then looked at Uraza lounging beside Abeke. His own hand stayed on Briggan's neck, buried in the fur.

"In my vision, I saw Briggan, Essix, Uraza, and Jhi in the battle with us. I saw . . . I saw Uraza overwhelmed by Conquerors, and Briggan's tattoo disappeared from my arm. Jhi was helpless, and Essix was nowhere at all."

Silence.

"I think . . ." Conor said slowly, as if unwilling to say the words aloud, "that our spirit animals may not survive this war."

PRISONER

THE PRISON DOOR WAS UNLOCKED.

It was always unlocked. Gerathon saw to it, because she knew that it made no difference for Meilin. She wanted Meilin to sit here, cowering against the wet, mossy dungeon wall of her prison cell, staring for hours at the door that taunted her with the freedom she knew she couldn't have.

Meilin wrapped her cloak more tightly around her and snuggled against Jhi's fur. She couldn't sleep. If she could see herself in a mirror, she knew there would be dark circles under her eyes. Whenever she did manage to sleep, she dreamed of her father. She would wake thinking that he was alive – alive! – somehow, maybe even here with her in this cell. But then the images from her dreams would fade away, and reality would settle heavily back into the pit of her stomach.

Her fingers played numbly with a sash tied around her waist. They had cut away her manacles. No point in escaping. She couldn't trust herself anymore, not in her current state. Even now, with Gerathon far off doing . . . whatever she did, Meilin could feel the subtle, menacing presence of *someone else* in her mind, coiled in the shadows and waiting to lash out when needed. She shuddered at the memory of the snake's domination—the helplessness of not being able to control her own limbs and actions. What would she do if she escaped the dungeons and went back to her friends, anyway? Betray them again?

"At least Abeke is free," she whispered under her breath. Abeke should have made it back to Greenhaven by now, with Shane in tow. Meilin couldn't understand Abeke's attachment to that boy, although a part of her sympathized, wondering how it must feel for Shane to have been used by the Conquerors—to watch his sister die like that. She hoped the Greencloaks had accepted him too, and that they were both safe now.

Beside her, Jhi made a deep sound in her throat that set her entire body humming. Meilin paused in her thoughts to look up at her panda. Jhi returned her gaze with wide dark eyes. She knew what the panda was trying to say.

Don't worry. The others will return for us. This won't go on forever.

"No," Meilin snapped for the hundredth time. She recalled Abeke and Shane leaving her, promising that they would return for her. She'd let them go. "They're not coming back. There's no point. I don't even think I want them to."

One look at Jhi's mournful gaze was enough to send guilt shooting through Meilin's heart. She patted the panda's fur. "I'm sorry. I didn't mean it like that." She sighed. "Oh, Jhi. What will happen to us?" She laughed a little, a sad sound. "Do you think . . . do you think the universe made a mistake, pairing the two of us together? Do you think it knew how I would treat you?"

When Jhi only made the rumbling sound in her throat again, sending soothing tremors through Meilin, she shook her head. *Maybe I wasn't supposed to have a Great Beast at all. But I'm glad I do.* She squeezed Jhi's side softly. Once, she would have forced Jhi into the passive state and kept her there, too annoyed to deal with Jhi's insufferably patient, sympathetic expression. Now, she couldn't imagine sitting in this cell without the panda's presence nearby. "Forgive me, Jhi. I'm just . . . so tired. So tired of not having my thoughts be my own."

Jhi licked her hand in reassurance. Meilin leaned against her, soaking in her familiar comfort, and closed her eyes. The image of Gerathon's smiling jaws and slithering body disappeared, replaced instead with Rollan's lopsided grin and Conor's encouraging voice, Abeke's clear laugh.

The prison door's hinges squealed. Meilin shot to her feet right as Jhi let out a low growl.

It was Shane.

He looked more tired than she remembered, the bags under his eyes dark and prominent, but it was still unmistakably Shane. His silhouette was stark against the opening of the cell, looking uninjured. His shirt was unbuttoned low into his chest, almost casually.

A surge of excitement and fear cut through her melancholy. Meilin could hardly believe her eyes – she didn't even know how to feel. For a moment, the two just stared at each other in complete silence.

Finally Meilin found her voice. "You came back . . ." she whispered.

Shane nodded. "I did."

They had come back to rescue her, after all.

In spite of everything, Meilin burst into a grin. She felt a sudden urge to hug him. The dark thoughts that had plagued her just a moment ago suddenly vanished. If Shane was here, then that meant he and Abeke had made it back to Greenhaven!

Abeke has reunited with the others.

It meant all sorts of things. The questions started to spill out of her before she could stop herself. "Is Abeke safe? Are there others with you? Did you come with Greencloaks? The east stairs of the dungeon are crawling with—"

"I'm here alone."

Meilin wrung her hands. She looked uncertainly around the cell. "How are we going to get out of here? And even if we do—if I go with you—Gerathon can still see and control everything." She gave Shane a determined look. "You shouldn't have come back. Just leave me here, and go help the others. I'll only make everything worse. I—"

Jhi's growl cut her sentence short. Meilin shot her a quizzical look. "What's wrong? It's just Shane." She glanced back to him. "Shane, we have to . . ."

Her words faded away. Meilin frowned, suddenly hesitant. Something seemed different about Shane's expression . . . in fact, something seemed off about this entire encounter.

"Shane?" Meilin said. "What's wrong?"

"Nothing's wrong," Shane replied. Even the sound of his voice seemed different – colder, somehow, a far cry from what she remembered. "I just came by to check on you."

Meilin raised a skeptical eyebrow. In the past, her instincts had always guided her thinking and actions. Even now, with her trust in her own perception shaken by the Bile, she wanted to rely on her gut feeling . . . and her gut was telling her that something was horribly off. A low growl continued to rumble from Jhi's throat. Meilin took a step back.

Then she noticed something peeking out from the opening of his shirt. Part of a dark mark. A tattoo? She frowned, focusing closer on it. Yes, it looked like . . . reptilian teeth, protruding from a jaw of scaly skin. She gasped. The rest of the tattoo disappeared inside his shirt, but Meilin didn't need to see all of it to understand.

The teeth and scaly skin belonged unmistakably to a crocodile. But a crocodile was *the Devourer's* spirit animal. . . .

Behind Shane, two Conquerors emerged in full armor. They saluted him as soon as they arrived. Meilin glanced back to him at the same time that he narrowed his eyes. "I came back to make sure you are still in your cell, and that you are well."

A million thoughts rushed through her mind. "Shane . . . ?" she managed to say. Impossible. It couldn't be. . . . A glint of metal from Shane's light blond hair caught Meilin's attention. She recognized the circlet she'd seen Gar wearing – a snake devouring its own tail.

"Yes. I'm the Reptile King." He lifted an eyebrow at her. "Are you really so surprised?"

Shane. The thought sank into her mind. Shane was the Devourer?

"Your wolverine . . ." Meilin gasped out, trying to make sense of it all. She glanced again at the tip of his tattoo, hoping that the second time around, she might see something different.

But the teeth and scales were still there. Like they'd been there forever.

"You . . ." Meilin said. "In Zhong, when —" She choked on her words, and it took her a second try to get them out. "It was you all along. *You* killed my father!"

Shane just shook his head. "Save your indignation," he replied, leaning against the wall. "It wasn't me in that armor at Dinesh's temple, it was my uncle. And Gar is dead. The Greencloaks killed him in Nilo, shortly after you saw him. Your revenge is complete. I've merely come to inform you that we'll set out soon, and you're invited to join us. I'm sure you'll want to come along."

Meilin's emotions warred against each other until she could hardly breathe. Gar was dead, but Shane — the true Devourer — had betrayed them. Somehow, that felt even worse. He had never wanted to help them.

What about Abeke?

She didn't make it back to Greenhaven, Meilin thought in horror. *She might even be dead*. The possibility that Shane had hurt her friend, the thought that Abeke . . . Blood rushed to her head, making her sway. The room spun for a moment. With the fear came a flood of rage. Meilin trembled from head to toe. With a furious cry, she hurled herself at him. She could feel the world around her slowing down as Jhi's abilities came rushing to the forefront — she saw Shane throw his arms up in defense, but the movement looked long and labored. Meilin balled up her fist. She managed to dodge past his arms and strike him square in the jaw. Shane staggered backward in slow motion.

"Jhi!" Meilin called out.

Jhi braced herself, then lunged for the boy too.

Then, abruptly, the coiled monster in the shadows of her mind reared its ugly head. Numbness froze all of Meilin's limbs. She gasped. The world, so slow a moment ago, suddenly sped up, rushing around her in a streaked blur. Meilin blinked, trying to keep up.

Shane darted backward — a thunderous roar echoed in the cell. Something green and brown and scaly flashed before Meilin's eyes. An instant later, she felt a tremor go through the floor and fell to her knees. Jhi halted in her attack. Meilin managed only to hold a hand up to her face and stumble backward. Her limbs felt detached and weak.

An enormous saltwater crocodile appeared between them and Shane, its legs as thick as tree trunks. Meilin gasped. The beast opened its jaws at Jhi, then slammed its tail down on the floor. Its eyes were slitted and shiny. They glinted with something savage, completely different from the warmth in Jhi's eyes.

Jhi nudged Meilin back, putting herself protectively between Meilin and the crocodile.

Shane brushed hair out of his eyes and sighed. "Call your panda into its dormant state," he said. "Now."

More fog seeped into Meilin's mind. She staggered, clutching at her head and trying in vain to fight off Gerathon's presence. The compulsion was as strong as ever. She felt herself putting out her arm, as if she were a

Zhongese puppet toy, opening her mouth to call Jhi back. Jhi cowered, lowering her head.

A memory came to Meilin of Abeke. Abeke, who could be in serious trouble right now.

No. Fight it.

With a mighty effort, Meilin gritted her teeth and tried to push back. Lights burst in her vision. Shane smiled at her as she struggled. One of his hands ran along the scales of his crocodile. "Abeke was right," he said. "You *are* stubborn."

The mention of Abeke gave Meilin more fuel. She clenched her jaw, bracing herself against the fog that threatened to take over. Her hand was still outstretched in Jhi's direction, but the commands halted on her tongue, clamoring for release.

No.

The lights across her vision grew, blinding her. She squinted as they erased her surroundings for a moment.

Was Jhi causing this? It all felt similar to the glowing orbs Meilin would sometimes see when Jhi helped her to make decisions calmly, but somehow . . . it was different too. This time, the light narrowed into a line across her vision, then centered as if she were staring down a dark tunnel toward something impossibly bright and warm. The golden path cut through the blue-gray haze of fog, of the Bile's whisper and poison. Meilin reached for the light.

The light pushed the fog back. Only for an instant.

Meilin withdrew her hand, refusing to call Jhi into her dormant state. Then she lunged at Shane once more.

Shane's eyes popped open in surprise. Meilin managed to strike a glancing blow against his cheek before his crocodile's tail caught her legs and sent her crashing to the ground. Shane drew his saber and pointed it at her throat. All hints of amusement were gone from his face.

"Chain both of them to the wall," he commanded. The two Conquerors waiting behind him moved immediately.

Meilin shook her head as she felt the soldiers pinning her hands against the cold stone of the wall, then clapping chains around her wrists. Her rebellion had already ended. Gerathon's coils slithered across her thoughts – in her mind, Meilin heard the Great Serpent chuckling. Beside her, the panda stared cautiously at the crocodile while a Conqueror secured her paws with manacles.

Poor little girl, Gerathon hissed inside Meilin's mind. *I'll have to be careful with you.*

Gerathon chuckled again, but somehow, Meilin thought she could detect a hint of wariness from the serpent. Somehow, in some way, Meilin had managed to *push back* against the Bile. It hadn't lasted long. But it had *lasted*.

Shane cast her one last look before calling his crocodile back. It vanished in a flash of light to reappear on his chest. He scowled. Meilin knew he would never admit it, but she could see that her moment of defiance had shaken him. As Gerathon lost interest in controlling her, she felt the fog dissipate from her mind and bring the prison cell back into sharp focus. Her anger returned with it.

Shane had been the Devourer all along. He fooled us.

"See to it that her door stays locked," Shane snapped at the Conquerors. Then he motioned for them to file out.

Meilin found her voice right as Shane was about to leave. "I don't know what you did to Abeke," she spit out, "but you don't deserve her. And if you hurt her, I'll make sure you pay for what you did."

Shane hesitated with one foot still inside her cell. He didn't turn around. Instead, his jaw tightened, and a strange emotion flickered across his face, something Meilin almost wanted to interpret as . . . regret.

The moment lasted barely a few seconds, and it passed so quickly that Meilin couldn't be sure he'd hesitated at all.

Then he stepped out of her cell, and the door shut with a loud, echoing clank.

Meilin sat in the new silence, savoring that echo, listening to the Conquerors' footsteps disappear down the hall. In spite of everything, she couldn't stop a small smile from creeping onto her face. Jhi blinked when she looked at her.

Gerathon had kept that cell door open to taunt her all this time, knowing she couldn't—*wouldn't*—escape.

But the door was locked now, because Meilin had *forced* them to do it. She continued to dwell on this. And she dared to hope.

5

OLD FRIENDS

THE FOLLOWING DAY, ALLIES WHO HAD RECEIVED AND accepted their call for help began to arrive, just as Olvan had said they would. Conor waited anxiously to see each of them cresting the horizon and approaching the castle in sporadic groups. It would be a long, hard road ahead for all of them, but at least they were in the company of old friends.

First came Finn, the Greencloak covered in tattoos who had helped the team find Rumfuss the Boar. Finn arrived in stoic fashion, leaner than before and quieter than ever, although he did manage to crack a small smile of greeting when he saw Conor, Abeke, and Rollan. At his side was Donn, his sleek black wildcat. The cat purred as they made their way back to Greenhaven Castle. Conor marveled at him, remembering the awe they all had felt when they first realized Finn's spirit animal was this legendary creature.

"And how has life treated you in Glengavin?" Abeke asked as they walked.

Finn shook his head. "Very well," he replied, "until last week."

"Why?" Conor asked. "What happened?"

"What a shame that we reunite under such circumstances." Finn's voice turned grim. "You'll recall our friend MacDonnell, yes? His castle, his law? Well, the Conquerors returned to Trunswick, this time in huge numbers, and laid siege. Lord MacDonnell was forced to retreat and leave his estate to the Conquerors. He will commit his soldiers to our cause."

Rollan made an angry sound in his throat. "Our week hasn't been great either," he said, pointing up at the dreary sky. "Although I'd much rather get soaked by rain than sacked by Conquerors."

Conor felt sad at the thought of the mighty lord's castle now overrun by Conquerors. Somehow, the older image of Lord MacDonnell in complete control of his domain was comforting. It seemed like such a long time ago. They'd only just learned that Zhong had fallen. Nilo had still been free. The Conquerors were moving fast now.

Next came Kalani, all the way from the islands of Oceanus, her cloak of seaweed now replaced with a standard cloak. She looked more irritated than Conor remembered, which he figured might have something to do with the fact that she was now in a place quite opposite to that of a tropical paradise. Still, she greeted Conor warmly, even as she muttered something about the never-ending cold drizzle.

"Thank you for coming, Kalani," Conor said with a smile. "It's good to see you."

"And you," Kalani replied. "It's only a matter of time

before the Conquerors take Oceanus completely. I didn't want to wait around for that to happen."

She greeted Abeke too, but when Rollan tried to say hello, Kalani's lips tightened and she looked away. Rollan's smile vanished as he did the same. It took Conor a moment to remember that Kalani still considered Rollan *tapu*—dangerous and forbidden—and therefore could not acknowledge him. This would make for an awkward journey.

As the day went on, Conor noticed that Abeke hovered constantly at the windows facing the harbors. He knew who she was searching for, and who she hoped to see. But they didn't come.

At the end of the day, only Maya and her fire salamander joined them, significantly less bothered by the chilly weather. Conor laughed in surprise at the sight of her. Maya looked nothing like she had when they'd last seen her, when she'd lain limp and nearly lifeless after unleashing the fury of her fire against the Conquerors. Her red hair had been burned away and her cheek scarred with a vicious wound. The scar was still there, a faint but permanent blemish, but Maya's red hair had grown back a little, enough for her to tuck it behind her ears, and a healthy pink glow illuminated her face. There was a weight in her brilliant blue eyes that didn't exist before, the lingering pain of the past . . . but time had a curious way of healing things, and Maya had managed to cover that burden with the new joy of seeing her friends again.

She squealed at the sight of them all, then threw herself into a hug with Conor, Abeke, and Rollan. Her fire salamander, Tini, watched from her shoulder, his bright yellow spots pulsing happily at the reunion.

"Other Greencloaks from Eura are on their way too," Maya told them as they headed toward the hall for dinner. Her short hair bounced with each step. "They'll join Olvan's forces." She glanced at Conor and nodded. "I'll go with your smaller patrol. You probably won't need any fire while traveling through Stetriol, but you'll certainly need a friendly face." She paused to look adoringly at her spirit animal. "And we are the friendliest faces, aren't we, Tini? Yes, we are!"

They all laughed. Seeing the old affection between the two of them lifted Conor's heart for a moment. It was really, *really* good to have Maya back.

The conversation over dinner stayed low. Conor felt like he could touch the tension in the air.

"A ship with other Greencloaks has set sail from Oceanus. They will join Olvan's forces in Stetriol." Kalani rubbed at her dolphin mark, the other tattoos lining her arms bold in the candlelight. Conor felt sorry for her that she couldn't call on her spirit animal in a place like this. She looked warily around the table. "Do we even know how to get to Kovo's prison, or the heart of Erdas?"

Olvan looked uncomfortable at the question, but he lifted his head authoritatively. "There are rumors of where Kovo's prison is. Ancient accounts of the first war tell of a chain of mountains in Stetriol, near which lies a formation called Muttering Rock. They say Tellun imprisoned Kovo there. Conor's visions of the red rock also support this theory. It will be a good starting point for us."

"We have some old maps," a voice called from the end of the table. A Greencloak named Dorian sat with them. Conor hadn't remembered seeing him around the castle.

He looked unpleasantly pale, with dark blond hair tied back in a short tail at the nape of his neck. His lips were thin and drawn back into a stern line.

Dorian laid out several parchments, faded and crinkling with age. He spread them flat on the table for everyone to see. "These are generations old, discovered in some ancient library texts." He pointed to a landmass on each that Conor had never seen before on any present-day map. "Stetriol."

Kalani didn't look reassured. Neither did Finn. He frowned at the older Greencloak. "This is all we have to go on? Visions? Rumors? Maps from hundreds of years ago? The world has changed much since then. This will hardly be reliable." He sighed and rubbed a hand over his face. "I mean no offense, Conor," he added, "and I know your dreams are crucial to this, but we are heading into true darkness. The very center of it."

Conor saw Abeke shiver visibly. When she noticed him looking at her, she looked away and reached for a piece of bread. Abeke tore it in half, the crust crackling as she went. "We'll be prepared," she said, trying to sound optimistic. "We'll have plenty of water and provisions with us."

Kalani frowned and rubbed harder at her tattoo. Conor wondered how much water a place like Stetriol might have. The sight reminded Conor of his dream, of how he'd stared and stared at his tattoo of Briggan until he couldn't see him at all anymore. *I might not have Briggan forever.* Just the thought sent a stab of pain through him. He buried his hand deeper in the wolf's fur.

"Do we know if Stetriol has any harbors?" Kalani asked. "How many people still live there?"

"We know very little of Stetriol," Olvan answered. It was not what anyone wanted to hear. The Greencloak furrowed his brows. "Abeke is right. We will prepare the best we can."

Conor swallowed hard. He was sitting in a room with the world's finest Greencloaks, and no one sounded confident about their mission. They were sailing into the unknown now, an untouched and forgotten land. Briggan and the other Four Fallen had died leading the Greencloaks into Stetriol. What would happen this time?

"Sending the Four Fallen blindly into Stetriol," Finn said, "and sending an army of Greencloaks as their diversion, to face the Conquerors . . ." His eyes were tragic. He met Olvan's stare and held it. "This is a suicide mission, Olvan," he said gently.

Conor could feel the dread that rippled through the room. He, Rollan, and Abeke all looked at Olvan, half expecting him to deny such a claim. But he didn't.

"We leave tomorrow, at dawn," Olvan finally replied, his voice very quiet.

The realization slowly settled into Conor's heart. This was it, the final stand. Tomorrow, they would leave Greenhaven. And they might never return.

In the silence that followed, Finn bowed his head. He put a hand flat on the table. "I'm ready," he said.

"Me too," Maya added.

"Me too," echoed Rollan and Kalani at the same time. It startled them, and they looked at each other in surprise before they remembered that they weren't supposed to acknowledge each other. Kalani quickly looked away again.

Conor chimed in too, followed by Abeke, and gradually, everyone at the table pledged themselves to the journey. They were all ready to lay down their lives. Conor looked around the room, memorizing the moment and the faces.

Finally Rollan grabbed another dinner roll and bit into it with determination. "Better eat up now, then. It'll be a hard road."

6

DORIAN

THE JOURNEY TO STETRIOL BEGAN UNDER A FRAGILE sheet of rain and fog, with the smaller of the two Greencloak groups heading out first. Abeke, Conor, and Rollan each rode separately on their own horses; Uraza walked beside Abeke's mount, while Briggan loped easily alongside Conor. Essix soared ahead, seeking out the harbor where the *Tellun's Pride* waited for them. Sacks of provisions bumped against each of their horses' hindquarters. Behind them came Maya and Kalani. Finn rode ahead, talking in a low voice to the Greencloak named Dorian, who had been tasked with leading the little troupe. Dorian was now pointing out something on one of the ancient maps he'd brought. On his shoulder perched his spirit animal, a horned owl.

"I'm not sure he's going to lead us in the right direction," muttered Rollan. His eyes were fixed on Dorian and filled with resentment. "And an owl? Really? Is his hoot going to scare the Conquerors away?"

"He's the keeper of the maps," Conor replied, clearly trying to keep their conversation reasonable.

But Abeke understood Rollan's impatience. Dorian had woken each of them up that morning by pounding on their doors and shouting, like a father chiding his oversleeping children. He galloped ahead now, as if he had always been their leader, as if Tarik had never existed.

Rollan snorted. It didn't seem like "keeper of the maps" impressed him much.

"Keep Briggan out, okay?" he said. One of his hands checked idly for the Coral Octopus looped around his neck. "It would be nice if we didn't have to save you from your dreams every other day."

Conor shot him a guilty look, then glanced at Abeke. "Got the Granite Ram?"

Abeke nodded, showing him the necklace that kept it securely against her chest. She tugged once on it, just to be sure. "You can hang on to it, if you want," she said.

Conor shook his head. "I'd rather not."

Abeke gave him a small smile. Even after all this time, he still seemed a little hesitant to be the one responsible for hanging on to a talisman. She stared at him for a moment longer as he turned his attention back to the trek. How different Conor looked from when they'd first started their journeys together – he'd grown taller, and lost the fat in his cheeks. Even Rollan, with all his jokes, had changed ever since he lost Tarik and donned the green cloak. He was more focused. More serious. The realization took Abeke off guard. How quickly they'd all changed.

Her thoughts wandered back to her father and sister, and whether their village in Nilo was truly covered in snow. Uraza turned her violet eyes up at Abeke, as if she could read the girl's mind. Abeke just smiled. "We're okay," she said. "I don't need them here." Then she turned away from her spirit animal, so Uraza couldn't tell that she'd lied.

Most of all, she didn't want Uraza to see how afraid she was that she might lose her.

By the time they reached the *Tellun's Pride*, the entire party looked like a pack of waterlogged rats in wet green cloaks. The ship's captain was already waiting for them at the pier, hollering at the top of his lungs at the crew hoisting crates and rolling barrels up the ramp.

He shook his head grimly as Finn and Dorian approached, then pointed down at the water. "Choppy, murky waters today," he muttered. "We'll have some rough seas to endure." He pointed to where taut ropes at the bow of the *Tellun's Pride* disappeared beneath the waves. "And the rockback whales — they may be sick."

"I'll check on them," Kalani said, shrugging her right shoulder, which housed her dolphin tattoo. She winced — light flashed briefly around her, and a moment later, everyone heard the unmistakable call of a dolphin from the water. Kalani leaned over the pier. Abeke was certainly no sea creature expert, but even she could tell that the dolphin was unhappy to be in this cold, unfamiliar ocean. She felt her heart tug at the sight of Kalani's brow furrowing in concern.

"See how the rockback whales are doing," Kalani called down to her dolphin. "Be careful."

The dolphin made a subtle nodding gesture before diving below the surface. They all waited for a few quiet minutes.

All of a sudden, the dolphin exploded from the surface of the black water with a strange, sickly sound. Kalani gasped. She leaned forward and held her arm out.

"Come back up!" she said.

The dolphin splashed around a bit more on its side. Light engulfed the creature before it vanished from the water and returned to Kalani's shoulder. Kalani swayed. Conor and Rollan had to rush forward to keep her from falling backward. Abeke felt sick to her stomach at the sight. She didn't want to imagine Uraza in that kind of agony.

Kalani finally turned to the captain. "The churning water has brought in some schools of tiny, poisonous fish. They are making the whales sick. We have to leave. Now. The whales won't survive if they continue like this."

"Is Katoa okay?" Abeke asked.

Kalani nodded with a tight mouth. "She's very sensitive to the water, even more so than the whales." She sighed. "With the sea around Oceanus also unhealthy, I haven't let her into the water in days. She's not happy."

Maya patted Kalani once on the shoulder. "Thank you for the warning," she said. "We better get moving."

"You heard her," the captain shouted to his crew, triggering another flurry of activity on the ship's deck. "Move out!"

Abeke walked up the ramp with the others. She tried not to look at the black water again.

7

DISRUPTION

T HE WATER TURNED LIGHTER AFTER THEY REACHED OPEN waters. Still, the air felt heavy and oppressive, in part, Abeke knew, because everyone felt a little bit anxious. Uraza's tail swished restlessly, and Abeke knew it wasn't just because they were on a ship—Uraza's least favorite form of travel. In fact, everyone's spirit animals seemed slightly on edge.

"Donn!" Finn shouted as he chased his black wildcat across the deck of the ship. Abeke and the others were in the middle of a lesson with Dorian on how to use the ship's cannons. Scampering barely in front of the wildcat was Maya's fire salamander, Tini, giving off indignant little squeaks every time the wildcat swiped his claws at him. Chasing Finn was Maya, her hair in complete disarray, as if she had just awoken from a nap.

Tini reached the end of the deck, then turned and hissed at the wildcat. Maya managed to catch up just in time to call for her salamander. "Into the dormant state with you!" she exclaimed. Tini obliged all too willingly.

"Sorry about that," Finn said breathlessly. He gave his wildcat a reproachful glare, while Donn gave him the same look in return. Abeke, Conor, and Rollan all looked on from the cannon they were crowded around while Finn straightened his clothes and tried to walk off in a dignified manner.

Rollan raised an eyebrow. "I would just like to point out," he stated, looking skyward, "that Essix has been on her best behavior."

"That's because she gets to fly," Conor said. He'd kept Briggan in dormant state for most of the journey so far.

"Hey, Essix isn't having the best time either," Rollan retorted. Overhead, Essix circled restlessly, making agitated little squawks. "She thinks the fish taste funny."

"All right," Dorian interrupted, nodding back down at the cannon. "Attention back there, all three of you."

As Dorian explained how to light the fuse once powder had been loaded into the cannon, Rollan gave him a mutinous look. Abeke tightened her lips. She shook her head at Rollan, warning him not to be so defiant to their new leader. Rollan remained silent, but the resentment stayed on his face.

As they sailed through the narrow sea dividing Eura and Nilo, they saw more that worried them. Where fertile farmland once thrived in southern Eura, enormous cracks now marred the parched, scorched earth left behind by invading patrols of Conquerors. Farmers gathered on the shore to watch them sail past, looking lost. Abeke wondered if they thought one of the passing ships could stop and save them, or perhaps take them far away to somewhere safe. Farther east, they passed entire cities that had been overtaken, their flags now gone and replaced with the Conquerors'.

"We must detour from our planned route," Dorian announced to everyone one morning as he studied his maps. "The Conquerors have seized an important trade strait between Nilo and Eura."

"Tarik would never have let us sail this far without knowing that," Rollan muttered under his breath. Abeke rolled her eyes at him. They'd just heard about the seizure that morning by messenger pigeon.

She pictured her homeland overrun by Conquerors, and could hardly bear the thought: the peppers and wild grasses burned away, razed by the invading soldiers. The antelope all migrating from the fighting. Would the lions and hyenas turn on the tribes in hunger? What would the people eat? What were the Conquerors going to do to them?

They docked that afternoon in Balanhara, a port city situated at the beginning of a thin strait between Nilo and Zhong, to restock their provisions.

It was a mistake.

"Look," Conor muttered to Abeke as they walked through the port's narrow streets behind Maya and Rollan. All of them were balancing barrels of water on their heads. Kalani had stayed behind to help on the ship. "Conquerors attacked this city."

The inner city still had some of its beauty – baskets and bags of colorful spices sat out in the open markets. Their smells were rich and enticing, reminiscent to Abeke of home. Bright glass trinkets hung from the crowded wooden stalls, reflecting the sunlight. But Conor was right. Once-beautiful homes were now pitiful structures of crumbling stone and broken wood. The harbor itself was almost completely destroyed by fire, with two of its piers washed entirely away.

Beggars crowded the alleys, their thin arms out-stretched. People paraded through the streets several times during their walk, the processions all in honor of the dead. Mourners hoisted the deceased on their shoulders in ominous white carriers.

Abeke looked away. So many funeral processions.

"All this couldn't have happened in just a week," she whispered to Conor.

Conor bent down to pick up a glittering tile fragment that had once belonged on the side of a building. He admired it sadly, holding it in the sunlight. "The Conquerors move fast," he muttered. He put the fragment carefully in his pocket, as if a reminder of what their mission was for.

Maya turned back to look at them. Her fire salamander stayed hidden behind her loose hair. "I just overheard a passerby. In the past two weeks, Balanhara suffered two sieges. The Conquerors finally passed through, but they left behind a trail of destruction. They've destroyed huge areas of the region." She paused to look sadly at the beggars. "A lot of victims."

As they passed more homes, Abeke saw that makeshift talismans hung on many of the doorways. The talismans were made out of barnacles, bits of broken clay, and beads. They were crafted in rough imitation of *real* talismans, the Coral Octopus and the Slate Elephant, the Marble Swan and the Silver Wolf, each dangling like a silent wish for help from the Great Beasts. Abeke's heart twisted.

"We have to do something," she said. But she didn't know what. Maybe all of this was because Kovo had already been freed from his prison—that they were too late. The thought made her shudder.

Rollan paused as they entered a small marketplace with food carts. The space looked like it usually held many more stands, but now only a few stood here and there. Most sold small, sallow potatoes and other roots that had survived the raids. Other stands sold rotten meat swarming with flies. Abeke guessed that the meat must have been salvaged from cattle killed during the siege. She wrinkled her nose at the smell, sickened by the reality that the people would be forced to eat such things.

The only cart selling something that looked good was situated at the far corner of the market. Abeke's stomach rumbled; they had all skipped breakfast in order to help out with gathering provisions, and now the sun hung high overhead. She joined Rollan's side to stare longingly at the golden-brown meat buns the vendor was frying over a flat iron disc.

"Let's pick some up for the others on the ship too," Conor said as Rollan pulled out a pouch of coins.

"Don't worry," Rollan replied, handing the money over. "I promise I won't eat all of them."

The vendor gave them bags of meat buns, and then they continued on their way. Abeke bit enthusiastically into hers. The food was delicious—the fatty juices spilled down her chin, the spices making her tongue tingle. She wiped her mouth with the edge of her sleeve. Conor was popping his last bite into his mouth, while Rollan had already finished one and was digging for another.

As they walked and ate, Abeke thought she could see a seagull following them from broken roof to broken roof, but it flew off every time she tried to look at it. She didn't dwell too much on it, though. They were in a port city, after all, and close to the water. The seagulls must be just as hungry as she was.

They turned into a filthy alley. What they saw made all of them pause in their steps.

Beggar children huddled here, their gray rags barely able to hide their skinny arms and legs. At first, they startled at the strangers. Then their eyes darted to the bags of food in their arms.

Abeke stared back at them, her appetite suddenly fading. These children were younger than they were—some much, much younger. Maya swallowed hard, her cheeks reddening. "Orphans," she whispered.

The children didn't dare make a move. Rollan was the first to break the stillness by bending down to a little girl. She shrank away from him. "It's okay," he murmured. "I remember living this life." Then he reached into his bag and pulled out a meat bun. He held it out to her. "Bet you're hungry."

The girl stared at him with wide eyes. She blinked at the food right in front of her face, still steaming hot. Then she reached out and hesitantly took it from Rollan's hand. They all looked on as she devoured the bun, as if she hadn't had real food in days.

The other children in the alley began to gather near them. Conor glanced at Abeke. "Give them our bags," he said in a quiet voice. "We'll buy more for ourselves." He stooped down beside Rollan and started handing the food out. Rollan gave him a grateful look. Abeke followed suit, as did Maya.

At the sight, the hesitant children suddenly surged forward, their outstretched hands everywhere. Their silence turned into laughter, smiles, and shouts. Abeke couldn't understand what they were saying, but their desperation was obvious enough. She handed out meat buns as quickly as she could, filling the empty hands. Still, more came. She realized that others begging outside the alley had gotten a whiff of what was happening. More crowded in, cutting them off.

"No more," Conor said as he held up an empty bag. But the people didn't see him, or perhaps they were too tired or hungry to notice.

One little boy pointed at the tattoo on Abeke's arm. He glanced back up at her. His eyes grew wide. "Uraza," he whispered.

Abeke shook her head quickly, trying not to draw more attention to them, but the boy had already turned back to the street. "The Four Fallen are here!" he yelled, pointing frantically at Abeke.

The words rippled through the crowd.

"We should get out of here," Conor said.

They started pushing their way through the alley. The sight of so many hungry faces tugged at Abeke's heart. If they failed in their mission, would the entire world become this? What would happen if the Conquerors won? The thought plagued her as their group finally made it out of the alley and started heading back toward the harbor. Behind them, a steady stream of beggars trailed along, some chanting and cheering.

The Four Fallen are here to save us!

"We've attracted too much attention," Maya said through gritted teeth. They surged on, trying to leave their followers behind. Still, Abeke thought she didn't look like she regretted anything.

The farther they traveled through the streets, the more people flocked in their direction. Abeke didn't think most of them could even tell whom they were cheering for— only that there was a commotion, and excitement, and a welcome distraction from the city's misery.

She winced as someone bumped her shoulder hard. They were surrounded by a blur of faces, over which she could see a sliver of the harbor beyond. Too many people. Abeke's heart began to beat faster, and she forced her rising panic down.

Something flashed past her line of sight.

An arrow hit the man closest to Abeke, right in the shoulder, and he screamed. The force of the hit sent him tumbling backward.

Instantly, the crowd broke into chaos.

Abeke dropped her barrel of water. The precious contents sloshed out and spilled all over the ground. Maya dropped down into a crouch.

"Forget the water!" Conor hissed. He grabbed Abeke's wrist and pulled Rollan close, abandoning their remaining barrels.

All around them, people fled in panic, a blur of motion and colors. Abeke could hardly see in the midst of all the flying dust.

Someone had just tried to kill her.

The seagull that had followed them came rushing back

to her thoughts. What if that was a Conqueror's spirit animal? The Conquerors had passed through not long ago.

Another arrow came whizzing from nowhere. It hit a nearby woman in the leg.

"Go!" Conor urged, pointing through the mass of panicking townspeople. He ducked into the thick of the crowd and pulled Abeke after him. The others followed. Screams filled their ears.

"Someone's firing from the roofs!" Rollan called out over his shoulder. He ducked lower. Abeke did the same, so that from the air they were all but invisible in the chaos. Abeke fought the urge to call for Uraza—this was no time to have their spirit animals out, drawing even more attention. She gritted her teeth and continued weaving through the people. She thought she saw a glimpse of blood on someone, but the image flashed past her too quickly to get a good look.

All they wanted was a bite of food. How did this get so out of hand?

By the time the four made it back to the port, their assailants had vanished. They were all panting. Maya rushed ahead to let everyone know that they had arrived. Rollan stopped to lean on his knees.

"Well," he muttered to Conor, "it's nice to know that good deeds are rewarded."

"The Conquerors must be hunting for us," Abeke replied as she leaned against a wooden post, struggling to catch her breath. "I saw a seagull following us. We need to get out of here before they catch up to us again. We don't have much time."

Conor and Rollan nodded silently. They hurried onto the deck of the *Tellun's Pride*, where Finn and Kalani waited impatiently for them. Kalani rushed over as soon as they were on board. "Are you all okay?" she asked. "We saw the commotion in the streets."

"We're okay," Conor replied, even though his expression didn't look like it.

Finn ushered them belowdecks immediately. Abeke nearly tripped on the ladder's steps in her haste.

Dorian was waiting for them in the hold. As they arrived, he straightened and frowned at them from behind his maps. In the sudden dark, Abeke had nearly mistaken him for Tarik, summoning a fresh pang of grief.

"What happened out there?" he asked. His owl was perched beside him on the table, watching the team with its own sharp gaze.

"The Conquerors attacked us when we . . . accidentally drew a crowd," Conor replied. Sweat beaded on his brow. He looked suddenly guilty. The floor beneath their feet was already shifting—the *Tellun's Pride* had just pulled away from the harbor.

"And what were you all doing, to attract such a crowd?"

Rollan's jaw tightened. "We passed through a narrow alley with children orphaned from the storms. I stopped to give a girl a meat bun."

Finn shook his head sympathetically. Beside him, Dorian gave them all a stern look.

"Good intentions," Dorian said. "But now's not the time for it."

Rollan rolled his eyes. Already, he looked like he was bristling at Dorian's presence. "Oh, come *on*. We're all safe and well, aren't we?"

Dorian pressed his lips into a line. "We must lie low,

and you're drawing too many eyes." His voice lowered. He looked at Conor, who hung his head. "Remember, the fate of Erdas lies in our hands. We cannot afford to be distracted from our primary mission by small acts of kindness."

Rollan couldn't seem to hold in his irritation anymore. He scowled. "It was my idea, not Conor's," he snapped. "So don't blame him,"

"Very well, then. I'll hold you responsible for putting your companions' and, indeed, all of our lives at stake."

"If we can't even bother to be kind to people in need, then what's the point of saving Erdas?"

Dorian frowned back. "Your actions drew the Conquerors' attention. Is that what you want?"

Rollan's voice grew louder. "*Tarik* would have been proud of us, if he was still here! But he's not. We just have *you*, trying to fill his shoes."

Dorian winced visibly at that. It lasted only for an instant before it was replaced with his stern look, but even Rollan seemed to recognize he'd hit a sore spot. He crossed his arms and dropped his gaze.

An awkward silence hung heavily in the air. Abeke searched Dorian's face for that vulnerability she'd seen before, but his eyes were every bit as fierce as his spirit animal's.

Truly, she felt a bit sorry for him. How must it feel to have to step into Tarik's shoes, to be the newest person in a group that had already bonded together over so much? She remembered that feeling well enough.

"Balanhara was our last dock," Dorian said, his voice cold. Clearly their prior conversation was over. "We won't stop again."

He turned his back and headed up the ladder with Finn. But before he left them, he paused and looked over his shoulder.

"Tarik and I joined the Greencloaks at the same time," he said. "We trained together. So don't tell me things I already know."

Abeke watched him go. They remained silent for a long moment afterward.

Rollan let out a slow breath. His shoulders hunched. "I know, I know. I shouldn't have said that," he muttered.

Abeke walked over to Rollan and patted him on the shoulder. "I'm glad we helped those children," she said. "Even though it caused a lot of trouble. At least they have full stomachs now."

Maya and Conor nodded their agreement. Rollan still looked unhappy, but his posture relaxed a bit, and he gave his friends a faint smile.

As they headed up to the deck to watch Balanhara fade away on the horizon, Abeke's thoughts wandered back to the seagull that had watched them before the attack.

Perhaps it was a coincidence.

BATTLE AT SEA

WHEN ROLLAN WENT UP TO THE DECK OF THE *TELLUN'S Pride* the next morning, the ocean had turned choppy and black. *Black.*

Not a normal color for the ocean, he thought to himself. He winced at the wind and huddled under his cloak. Everyone else was still asleep belowdecks, except for the few crew members manning the sails. He took a deep breath.

His anger and guilt over what happened yesterday had faded away into a sullen understanding. Dorian was right, of course. Rollan just didn't want to admit it. When he next saw Dorian, he would apologize for what he said.

Essix glided somewhere overhead. Rollan turned his face skyward, searching for her, but all he saw were churning clouds. It seemed like the entire world had been stripped of color. Even the whales pulling the *Tellun's Pride* forward seemed uneasy, blowing enormous plumes of mist into the air. Rollan grimaced at the ominous water, then squinted out toward the horizon.

It took him a moment to realize that another Greencloak was up on the deck besides himself. Kalani. She saw Rollan approaching and looked away quickly, toward the ship's bow.

"Good morning," Rollan said as he joined her. He glanced at the sky again. "Or not. What are you doing up so early?"

Kalani leaned over the railing, the edges of her mouth turned down.

Rollan sighed. "Look, I know that I'm officially poisonous to your people now, but if we can't even talk to each other on this mission, it's going to get us into trouble."

Kalani's eyes remained focused on the sea's surface, and Rollan realized she was searching for her dolphin in the waters. Maybe she was still weighing whether or not to acknowledge him. When she stayed quiet, he shook his head.

"Fine," he said. "I get it. But, Kalani . . . this may be the last journey we ever make together. I don't even know if we'll all come back." His voice lowered. "And if we *don't* make it back . . . do you really want our last days together to be spent like this?"

At that, Kalani's stare finally shifted from the ocean to Rollan. She studied his face. He could see the conflict in her eyes. For a moment, he thought she might keep pushing back.

But then her shoulders relaxed, and she let out a long breath. Her eyes went back to the sea. "The whales aren't doing well," she said. And despite the severity of her words, Rollan couldn't help exhaling in relief. They were talking again. "I couldn't sleep because I could sense the distress of their underwater calls. So I came up here. Look." She pointed to the quivering ropes latched to the whales. "Their pace has slowed. They're sick. I sent Katoa to check on them."

So the whales *were* behaving oddly. Rollan didn't like the sound of that at all. If their whales were sick, they wouldn't be able to make it to Stetriol in time. They'd have to dock again somewhere. But they were so close! No other ports lay between here and Stetriol—nothing but open ocean. Where would they go?

"We've got to be getting close by now," Rollan muttered. Then he raised his voice. "Hey, Essix!"

A piercing cry answered him, muffled by wind and distance. Now he saw her—she hovered in a wide circle several hundred yards away from the ship. Her relaxed glide calmed him somewhat.

Between the surprise attack at Balanhara, his argument with Dorian, and now the whales' condition, Rollan could use a moment of calm.

When he looked back at Kalani, he could see tears welling in her eyes. Down in the water, her dolphin surfaced, whistling and clicking for her. She held out her arms and called it back into the dormant state before looking at Rollan.

"The whales," she murmured. "They're . . . dying. The waters here are slowly poisoning them."

"Dying?" Rollan said. He hadn't thought it would be as bad as that. The word seemed so final—the thought of their faithful rockback whales sacrificing themselves because of this journey hit him hard in the heart.

Kalani nodded. Her voice sounded flat and dead. "We need to cut them loose, if we want to save them. They need to get away from Stetriol to cleaner waters."

Rollan pulled out his long dagger. "Well, if you need a hand in cutting them loose . . . I'm in."

Kalani looked at the dagger with a pensive expression. Then she smiled weakly. "Thanks, Rollan. And . . . I'm sorry. I know you broke our customs for the good of Erdas, and that seeking Mulop cost you much. As a queen, I suppose I should be willing to do anything to save my people. Even become *tapu* myself." She sighed. "Let's go tell the captain."

The last word had barely left Kalani's lips when Essix sent up a shrill shriek. The sound penetrated the air like a knife, making Rollan jump.

"Okay," he said, "*that* didn't sound good." He searched the sky to see what made her give a warning cry. But the surface of the sea was covered with a layer of mist, hiding whatever else might be beyond.

"Hey."

Rollan turned to see Conor emerge from the lower decks. The other boy stopped beside Kalani and squinted first at the ocean, then up to the Greencloak observing the sea from the crow's nest. "What's Essix calling about?"

Rollan shrugged. In the mist, he could hardly make out Essix at all. "No idea."

"Think you can see through Essix's eyes for us?" Kalani asked.

Rollan looked back out at the ocean and concentrated. He felt the familiar experience of the world rushing at him, and the curious sensation of being airborne, of soaring over the dark water and through the mist. The air smelled sharply of salt and fog, and tiny droplets of water dotted his face.

Essix swooped down, then expanded her wings to their full length and caught the air currents. Rollan could feel the wind ruffling through her feathers. Everything looked a hundred times sharper than what he could see through human eyes.

At first, Rollan didn't notice anything unusual.

Then he saw the faint silhouette of a landmass looming behind the fog.

Essix shrieked again. Rollan rushed away from the sky and down toward the ship. He jolted back into his skin, right as he lifted his arm in the direction of the land and shouted, "Stetriol, straight ahead!"

A few seconds later, the lookout in the crow's nest called out the same thing. As others began emerging from belowdecks, Conor and Kalani stood next to Rollan and leaned out to see better. No doubt about it.

Jagged gray rocks rose from the horizon. Even from here, and even shrouded in mist, the vision sent a chill down Rollan's spine. He could *feel* something poisonous here, in the very air of the place. It didn't seem like so long ago when they had first passed Stetriol by.

This time, we will actually set foot on forbidden land. Was Meilin here?

As they drew closer, the land began to take on more detail, until Rollan could make out some sort of bay straight ahead. The wind began to pick up, and white foam crashed against jagged rocks lining the mouth of the bay. Some of the rocks glowed red with lava, still fresh and hot from the mouths of underwater volcanoes. These were pieces of land just days old, with new lava still flowing over them. The red-hot liquid gave the rocks the look of a giant beast's bloody jaws.

"There's no way we can squeeze through that without wrecking ourselves," Conor said grimly.

"I'm not sure we have much of a choice," Rollan replied. Indeed, the Greencloaks were already busy lowering the ship's masts, preparing to enter the strait. A harsh gust of wind nearly lifted Rollan clear off his feet. Overhead, Essix had returned to circling the ship. Her cry echoed again.

"Why is she still calling?" Conor shouted.

The ship lurched to one side as they drew closer to the stormy bay. Now they were near enough to hear the waves smashing themselves furiously against the rocks. The whales pulled hard as the Greencloaks urged them on. Kalani winced, and Rollan knew she could feel their agony.

Kalani looked worried. "The whales are exhausted," she said, "but they're going to try to get us through. It won't be an easy passage." She removed her cloak and stepped up onto the ship's railing. "I'm going to guide them, and then cut them loose. Make sure to hang on!"

"Right!" Rollan called back.

Then she jumped overboard, falling in a graceful arc and splashing into the sea. A moment later, she emerged perched on the back of her dolphin, hanging on to its fin.

Rollan was about to call up to Essix when he felt the world rush around him again. This time, he saw through her eyes to the ocean behind them. There, in the wavering

V that their ship had just carved through the ocean, came the shadow of *another ship*.

A Conqueror ship was hot on their trail.

Rollan felt his chest heave at the sight. Essix had been trying to warn them of something else all along, in addition to the jagged harbor they were about to enter. Now she turned her head forward, and Rollan saw why the other ship was here.

Right in front of Essix flew the seagull that had followed them in Balanhara. He could see it now through the mist, wind blowing through its tail feathers. *The seagull*, Rollan realized. *The Conquerors were watching us.*

Essix let out a sharp, angry cry and lunged for the bird.

Rollan gasped as his vision returned to him, and then grabbed Conor's arm. "Conquerors!" he shouted.

Now the Greencloaks were pointing at the ghostly ship too. The *Tellun's Pride* lurched again, sending sea mist spraying into their faces. No question about it – the Conquerors were frighteningly close, hidden from view the whole way by the thick mist. They would catch up in a matter of minutes.

"To the cannons!" the captain shouted.

They all leaped into action. Rollan and Conor ran to man a cannon. They were so close to the jagged rocks now. As the ship started to careen past the first rock, orange light burst from the Conqueror ship. Cannonballs! Rollan stumbled and fell to his knees as the first one made impact. The entire ship shuddered. Greencloaks ran by, some to douse the fire, others to the riggings. Still others were loading their own cannons. Rollan saw Dorian manning his own station while overseeing those closest to him.

"Fire!" Rollan heard Dorian's order shouted over the chaos. A volley of cannonballs sailed toward the Conquerors' ship, exploding in showers of splinters wherever they made contact.

Rollan gritted his teeth as he and Conor picked up a cannonball and staggered with it toward their cannon. Dorian's earlier lesson with them rushed through Rollan's head. He hated to admit it, but the instruction was about to come in handy. They shut the metal breech, then lit the fuse.

"Point it higher!" Conor urged as they turned it toward the enemy's ship.

"I know, I *know*!" Rollan snapped. "This thing's a lot harder to move than it looks!"

The fuse finished burning, and the cannon rocketed backward.

The recoil knocked Conor and Rollan off their feet. For a second, Rollan thought that the impact might have knocked all the teeth out of his mouth. He landed with a thud on his back. He struggled to catch his breath as he scrambled back up.

They were *much* too close for comfort. Rollan could make out the faces and expressions of the enemy crew, and even distinguish the details on the Conquerors' clothing. He glanced wildly across the deck and noticed Abeke and Finn manning one of the other cannons. Maya leaned over the railing, Tini on her shoulder, and focused on the enemy's ship. Fire burst from her hand, but they were still too far away for her to hit.

The ship shuddered again.

This time, they careened wildly. "Hang on!" Conor yelled, right before the side of the ship rammed into one of the bay's sharp rocks.

Hanging on was useless—Rollan went flying. His back hit the ship's railing, sending a shock of pain rippling through his body, robbing him of breath for an instant. The *Tellun's Pride* groaned in protest. Seawater flooded the deck, soaking Rollan's boots. The icy coldness of it made him cringe.

"I'm cutting the whales free!" Kalani's voice rang clear and high over the sound of crossfire and crashing waves.

Rollan leaned over as far as he could without toppling right off the ship. "No, wait—!" he started to shout.

But Kalani hoisted a long, gleaming dagger, leaped onto one of the whales' backs, and ran down its length on light feet. The sight sent a wave of flashbacks through Rollan, of when Meilin had done something similar.

Kalani sawed through one of the whale's restraints, then another. The ship lurched heavily, and another wave of salt water flooded the deck. Behind them, the Conquerors increased their fire. Kalani hacked at a water-logged rope. Finally she cut through one last restraint— and the first rockback whale broke loose with a tug. The creature immediately disappeared beneath the waves.

The ship's stern surged up with the sudden freedom, causing the second whale's harnesses to snap. The whale spouted a tall column of sea spray into the air before following its companion into the sea.

The *Tellun's Pride* was floating alone now.

More cannon fire. The ship shuddered, her wounded boards groaning under her own weight. Rollan squinted through crashing water to see the Conquerors' ship sailing past their stern, frighteningly close. Maya leaned over the railing of the *Tellun's Pride* to aim once again.

This time, her fire hit true. A ball of flames exploded upon impact with the enemy's deck, in a plume of gold, blue, and white. Wood, metal, and Conquerors went flying through the air and into the ocean.

Rollan's eyes shot to the unmanned helm of the *Tellun's Pride*. Where was the captain? As the thought flew through his head, he noticed the man lying unconscious on the deck. *Oh, no.* His eyes darted back to the helm. The ship shuddered again. They would never make it to shore.

An idea struck him.

He nudged Conor and made a sharp turning motion with his hands. Conor looked toward the helm too. His eyes suddenly lit with understanding, and his lips parted as if to repeat aloud what Rollan was thinking. They both hesitated, knowing how extreme their plan was—but only a few seconds. Conor nodded without a word, then started stumbling across the deck with Rollan in tow. The two boys reached the helm right as the ship shook again, bringing them once more to their knees.

From across the ship came a piercing whistle. Rollan glanced over to see Abeke swing her arms wide, as if to ask what they were doing. He made a wild gesture with his arms. "Abandon ship. Abandon ship!" he mouthed.

Abeke blinked, then immediately shouted to the people on either side of her.

Conor grabbed the helm and started to pull it toward

him with all his strength. Rollan did the same, throwing his weight into it. But their combined strength wasn't enough to turn the entire ship. They clenched their teeth, sweating and dripping with seawater.

"Let me help you boys out," a white-haired Greencloak muttered as he rushed over to their aid. It took Rollan a moment to realize that the man was Finn. Together, all three threw their might against the helm.

The ship turned sharply to the right—its nose headed straight into the enemy ship's side. *Suicide*, Rollan thought.

The two ships rammed into each other.

The *Tellun's Pride* sandwiched the Conquerors' ship against the jagged rocks of the bay. Wood splinters flew through the air. The impact jolted everyone off their feet. Rollan's head slammed hard into the deck. For an instant, the entire world blurred—sounds muffled and everything went dark. He fought against the encroaching blackness. *No, I can't lose consciousness right now!* High above him, he heard Essix's piercing war cry. She was trying to keep him awake.

Then he felt a hand grab his shirt and haul him to his feet. Conor threw an arm around him. "We have to jump!" he was yelling. "Can you hear me, Rollan? *Jump!*"

Rollan reached blindly for the railing. His hand connected with slick wood, and he carefully hoisted himself up. His feet dangled over the edge. The ocean churned beneath him, all darkness and fire and broken wood. *We're too high up!* But Conor's shouts rang in his ears, and he felt the other boy tug sharply on his arm. With a deep, shuddering breath, Rollan launched himself from the side. Air and glittering water rushed all around him, parting for him as he plummeted like a stone. The fall seemed like it took an eternity. Then he hit the water.

The icy cold of the sea knocked all the breath out of him. He floundered helplessly, not knowing top from bottom, where he was, or how to get to the surface. The distant, blurred noise of fighting, fire, and breaking of wood rumbled somewhere around him. Rollan had the sudden notion that this was how he would die.

What would happen to Essix if he did?

A talisman bumped against his chest in the water. He realized that the Coral Octopus was looped around his neck. Rollan reached desperately for it. His fingers closed around it, and suddenly he could breathe. He blinked, looking around in the water.

Abeke was struggling nearby.

Rollan swam toward her. He grabbed for her hand, lacing his fingers with hers, and then turned up toward the surface and kicked as furiously as he could. He tugged Abeke with him.

They surfaced with a terrible gasp. Suddenly the noise around him was deafening. He saw the wreckage of two ships, both in flames, crumbling slowly into the sea.

Conor waved a hand at them from several dozen feet away. Maya was already in front of them, Tini clinging tightly to the top of her head.

Abeke spit water from her mouth, then wiped a hand across her face. She turned toward land. "This way!" she shouted.

"Hang on to me," Rollan shouted back, submerging again. With the Coral Octopus's help, he was able to swim without surfacing as Abeke gripped his shoulders, floating along above him.

Conquerors and Greencloaks alike struggled in the choppy waves. Some fought each other. A few screamed.

Rollan saw a dark shape swim by. Chills ran down his spine. The fish was hideously lumpy and discolored, with red-and-black spots. Its sides were adorned with vicious, spiky fins. It swam between the struggling legs, disturbed by the churning debris. An explosion issued from the Conquerors' ship, sending tremors through the water. Rollan could feel the heat of the fire, even submerged in the cold water. He didn't dare look back.

I'm so tired. His waterlogged clothes threatened to pull him under. But still, he kept kicking, kept swimming. Abeke hung gamely on to his shoulders. Muffled shouts came from every direction.

Rollan had no idea how long they were in the water. Somewhere up ahead, he saw Kalani swimming through the murky blue, hanging on to one of her dolphin's side fins while Conor clung to the other.

Finally Rollan saw land underneath him. Moments later, his feet hit sand. He dragged himself through the surf, then collapsed onto the beach. His breath came in ragged gasps. Beside him, Conor rolled over onto his back and closed his eyes for a moment, his chest rising and falling rapidly. Abeke coughed up water nearby.

"Are you all right?" Kalani said as she hopped onto the sand and crouched down to them. Her dolphin leaped once in the water, then vanished in a flash of light to return to her shoulder. Around them, others were crawling onto the beach too. More Greencloaks fought with the few Conquerors on the sand who had survived the explosion and the ocean. Rollan looked on in exhaustion as the last Conqueror was finally defeated.

None of them said a word. They could only look back at where an inferno had completely engulfed the dying *Tellun's Pride* and the Conquerors' ship. Both were locked together and sinking slowly as the waves crashed them mercilessly against the rocks. Smaller fires dotted the water.

"Dorian!"

Rollan suddenly recognized one of the Greencloaks struggling through the sand beside him. The man collapsed onto his back as Rollan crawled to his side. Aside from multiple wounds and cuts from wood splinters, Dorian's face was ghostly white and his lips had turned a deep shade of purple. He trembled from head to toe. The exposed skin of his arms and legs was an unnatural color, covered with angry red welts.

Rollan looked up at Kalani as the others joined him. "What's wrong with him?" he said frantically.

Kalani just shook her head. "Poison," she replied. "From stonefish stings. If Stetriol's stonefish are anything like what I saw back home, he is in a great deal of pain. He must have swum right into one."

Dorian coughed, the sound terrible and raspy. He tried to focus on Rollan hovering above him, but he couldn't seem to see very clearly. Whatever words he tried to speak were too garbled to understand. Rollan struggled to say something, anything, to comfort him, but all he could do was stare. The vicious-looking fish he'd seen in the water returned to his mind.

Dorian drew one last, shuddering breath. Then he slowly went still.

Rollan sat back in the sand, stunned.

"I'm sorry," he mumbled. Then, louder. *"I'm sorry!"* He repeated it several times until he was shouting it. Abeke finally reached for his hand and told him gently that Dorian couldn't hear him.

Conor lowered his head and closed his eyes. Kalani murmured over the fallen Greencloak's head. "From the sea we came," she said, "and to the sea we return."

Overwhelmed, the small group sat on the beach and looked out to where the ships had both already disappeared from view. No more people struggled in the water. No Conquerors, no Greencloaks. A small handful of their original crew had survived and made their way to the beach, but it was a tiny number. And now the *Tellun's Pride*, which had carried them all so faithfully on so many voyages, had taken her last breath too.

Rollan swallowed hard. They made it to Stetriol . . . and there was no turning back.

GRAY HILLS

As the few remaining supplies that had washed to shore were salvaged, Conor gathered around Finn with Abeke and Rollan. The elder Greencloak had taken charge after Dorian's death. Altogether, their already small party now numbered only a dozen. Everyone else had perished. Conor noticed a few of the Greencloaks crying over the limp bodies of their spirit animals. A stoat, a blue jay, a lynx. He also saw a few animals fleeing into the underbrush. Spirit animals that must have lost their beloved human partners. The sight weighed down his heart.

One look at Finn's face was all that Conor needed to get a sense of their chances. The man's eyes were bleak, almost as dark as the inky ocean. He carried out the grim job of taking the old maps of Stetriol from Dorian's body, where they were still rolled up and tucked at his belt. Beside him, Donn hung his head and nuzzled Finn's leg in mourning.

"We need to head into the nearest village," he said to the small group gathered around him. He pointed down at the waterlogged map. "If there are any. There were once settlements on this coast, but that was a long time ago."

"What if we can't find any?" one of the Greencloaks asked. His voice was choked with tears. Conor had seen the man earlier, crouched in anguish over the body of the lynx.

Finn tightened his lips. "We have no choice but to find one. We do not have enough supplies to last us for more than a few days, and we need horses."

"And water," Conor piped up. "Don't we?"

"Yes, Conor," the man replied. "We barely have any water left, other than the canteens strapped to our belts. There's no time to lose." He paused, looking out into the churning seas. "But first, we'll pay our respects."

The sand was too wet to bury Dorian—and, it seemed to Conor, too disrespectful. Lowering fallen Greencloaks into pits half-filled with dark, icy water was no burial at all. Instead, Kalani and her spirit animal helped gather up large segments of wood that had broken from the body of the *Tellun's Pride*. They eased their fallen companions onto the boards, spreading their green cloaks neatly beneath them. They placed small tokens on each of the dead's chests. For Dorian, Conor chose the glittering tile fragment he'd found in Balanhara.

For the first time since they'd boarded the *Tellun's Pride*, Conor called for Briggan. The wolf appeared beside him in a flash of light. His great head turned, surveying the tragic scene. He stared for a long moment, then lowered his head and leaned against Conor's hand. He uttered a low, mournful whine. It seemed as if Conor could feel Briggan's grief through the wolf's fur. Uraza had emerged beside Abeke too, looking on, her pose subdued. Essix sat quietly on Rollan's shoulder, her expression fierce. Rollan's eyes stayed downcast in grief and guilt.

As Finn spoke words of respect for each, Conor glanced at Rollan from the corner of his eye. His friend's hand stayed wrapped tightly around the Coral Octopus hanging at his neck. Rollan looked like he was holding it together well enough, but Conor could tell he was thinking of all the things he'd said to Dorian.

He walked over to Rollan, then put a hand on his shoulder. "Hey," he said softly. Rollan startled, looking up at him. "We're going to win this war. We'll make Dorian proud."

Rollan looked back down at the Greencloak's still figure. "Yeah," he replied, although he didn't sound like he believed himself.

Conor wished he could see into the future, that he could have a dream that told him everything would be okay. But his mind remained clouded and uncertain. He'd always known their journey would be full of danger, but even after the attack at Balanhara, even after *everything* they'd all been through, it had still seemed like they would find a way.

Now he wasn't so sure. What if they all died in the uncharted lands of Stetriol, before they could even find Kovo's prison? Before they could rescue Meilin? If the Conquerors had already swept through so many cities, and the lands were starting to shudder from the shadow falling over them, then what would happen if Gerathon and Shane managed to free Kovo? What would be left?

Nothing. The answer that echoed in his thoughts made him shudder. *Nothing would be left.*

He could not allow that to happen.

Finn's last words faded away over the final body. A brief silence fell over everyone. Then they pushed each board out into the sea, watching from the shore as their friends floated out across the water on the broken strips of their beloved ship. Conor murmured a farewell under his breath.

They belonged to the sea and sky now.

"I can see why they wiped this place off the maps," Rollan muttered. "Not exactly a dream destination, is it?"

They had spent the entire day chopping their way through dry, brittle underbrush and a dying forest. Now, as they finally emerged on the other side, they saw a desolate, yellow expanse of plains spread out before them, with a small village situated at the bottom of bare foothills.

Conor had to admit—Stetriol didn't look like a country that anyone would visit voluntarily.

"Hide your cloaks," Finn said to all of them. "Greencloaks will not be welcome here."

Conor and Abeke removed theirs, but Rollan hesitated. His fingers fiddled with the clasp of his cloak. Conor remembered that it was not Rollan's cloak, but Tarik's.

"Tarik once told us never to take our cloaks off to win favor," Rollan mumbled. "In Boulder City."

Finn walked over to where Rollan stood. He gave him a sympathetic nod. "Wise words," he said gently. "But he will be with you now, cloak or not, just as you will always be a Greencloak."

Rollan nodded. Still, his eyes stayed down. "Yeah, you're right." Finally he unhooked the clasp. The cloak fell to the ground in a heap, sending up a shower of dirt. Rollan immediately bent down, picked it up, and started shaking dust from it. Conor looked on as Rollan folded the cloak carefully. He packed it tightly into his bag.

As the first town came into view, Conor was struck by how gray and brown everything looked. A long, low wall surrounded the cluster of homes, but the wall's rocks were chipped and crumbling. Some parts of it had collapsed entirely. The land around the town was dry and sparsely dotted with weeds. A couple of mules pulling carts of supplies waited at the wall's rusted entrance gates. The animals' hides were dull and dappled with sores, and Conor could see their ribs.

They entered the town quietly after the mules and their carts. The two guards stationed at the gates didn't look like guards at all, Conor thought, but merely poor peasant farmers in tattered tunics and shoes. As the Greencloaks walked in, he thought the two farmers cast them sidelong glances.

Conor looked away and instinctively scanned the sky for birds. He hadn't forgotten Balanhara yet.

"Don't worry," Rollan said, pointing up at Essix. "If any bird looks suspicious, Essix will make a lunch out of it."

"Lucky, being allowed to keep Essix out," Abeke muttered at Rollan. "I wish I could let Uraza prowl around, but Finn said it's too dangerous for her to be seen here. People might pass the word to the Conquerors that the Four Fallen have arrived."

Conor wished he could let Briggan out from his dormant state too—he missed the silent comfort of his presence.

Rollan just shrugged. "Now that you mention it, where are the Conquerors? I figured this place would be swarming with them."

"Maybe Shane is already gathering their entire army near Kovo's prison," Conor whispered.

Faded tavern signs with the town's name swung in the breeze. *"Gray Hills,"* read Abeke. As their small group wandered through the marketplace – or what Conor could only assume was a marketplace – the people walking past them averted their gazes, keeping their hats pulled low and mouths tight in thin lines. Once, Conor accidentally brushed the arm of a passing woman. The woman cringed as if he'd burned her, then hunched her shoulders and walked away as fast as she could.

Abeke stopped to smile at a little boy with dirty cheeks who stooped at the entrance of an alley, quietly watching them pass. As she did, the boy sneered at her, then spit in her direction before running off. She watched him go with her mouth open.

"With my remarkable powers of perception," Rollan said beside her, "I'm getting the very subtle hint that people might . . . possibly . . . not like us here. But it's hard to tell."

Abeke raised an eyebrow at Rollan's sarcasm, then returned to looking around the nearly deserted marketplace. "Why does everyone look so hostile? Like they think we're going to hurt them?" A few yards away, Finn and several other Greencloaks stopped at a corral to haggle over the prices of horses. "I'd understand if Uraza was prowling around, but it's not as if our spirit animals are out."

"I wonder if they can tell that we're Greencloaks," Conor whispered back.

The three made their way over to the corral. The owner, a man in ragged clothes, showed Finn his meager stable of horses. Even here, right in the middle of a business transaction, Conor could tell that the horse dealer was trying his best to not meet Finn's eyes.

The elder Greencloak handed over a small pouch of coins and came back with several horses. None looked healthy. They seemed to Conor not unlike the mules they'd seen entering the town earlier. He patted one horse's muzzle sympathetically, and it grunted in return.

As they led the horses away, Finn leaned down to them and said in a low, gruff voice, "Keep your wits about you. We're not staying long. The people fear us, because they think we might be Conquerors in disguise, spying on them."

"Conquerors in disguise?" Conor said.

"Apparently some Conquerors have been doing that to the border towns, to make sure the people stay meek and obedient. The towns are afraid of anyone they don't recognize."

Abeke exchanged a look with Rollan. "They keep their own people in a state of fear?" she said in a low voice. Then she glanced around. Conor followed her gaze, wondering with an uneasy feeling whether any of these townspeople were Conquerors in disguise, watching them.

Finn nodded. "Some have been whispering that a patrol of Conquerors came through here less than a week ago. We aren't far behind them." He sighed. "They took a great deal of the town's few food stores with them, as well as precious water supplies. There's not much left for us to purchase from anyone."

The thought unsettled Conor. Without water, they would run into trouble in the Stetriolan deserts in no time. "Do we have *any*?"

"Some," Finn replied. He looked across the market-place, where two Greencloaks were tying provisions to the backs of their horses. "Not much. We'll need to make good time. They say this village is the only one for miles."

Miles . . . with nothing but desert surrounding them. Conor could feel his throat turning dry at the very thought. If this mission failed, and they all perished in the waste-lands of Stetriol, it would be his vision that led them out here.

Finn saw Conor's expression and put a gentle hand on his shoulder. "We all chose this," he said in a lowered voice. "And we're going to follow you, Abeke, and Rollan to the end."

Conor straightened as much as he could. He lifted his chin. "Thank you," he replied.

They stayed in Gray Hills for the night, renting rooms in a small, cramped inn near the edge of the town. Conor shared a room with Abeke, Rollan, Maya, and Kalani. Despite the fact that the five of them were all squeezed into the cramped space, the real reason Conor couldn't sleep was because of the shifting colors in the night sky.

Sometimes it would be pure black, like a night sky should be. Other times, it would blaze scarlet, the tint of blood. As he looked on, the colors faded into blue, then an ominous brown. Conor wondered if they were visions — something only he could see. The sky didn't seem to wake the others. Briggan, out of his dormant state for the night in order to keep watch over Conor, kept his head turned up to the sky too, silently observing.

In the morning, the bodies of red-crested birds littered the streets.

No one opened their doors to greet them as the team checked their horses and left. The entire place had turned into an eerie ghost town. Conor shivered as they filed out through the town's exit gate and into the desert. Even though the land beyond was dry and desolate, he was still glad to leave Gray Hills.

As they rode, the land around them gradually changed from parched yellow plains to sandy red rock dotted with shrubs, the stone carved into rivulets where ancient water used to flow. Off in the distance, they could see the faint silhouette of the Red Mountains, a thin line of jagged rock running along the horizon. Their progress was sporadic, slowed down by the fact that Finn was constantly searching the maps for recognizable landmarks.

"Did your visions show you anything specific?" Abeke asked him as they rode side by side. "Nothing about the Conquerors chasing us, or the birds falling from the sky? The weird villagers?"

Conor shook his head. "The most specific thing I saw was a barren land and the trunk of some enormous tree. I know that Tellun, Kovo, and Gerathon were there. And all of us." He paused there. "Tellun was fighting on our side. I hope that means we'll encounter him soon."

Abeke's jaw tightened. "Some just prefer to stand by," she said quietly, "until they can't stand by anymore. Maybe Tellun's like that too."

"Did your visions ever tell us anything about oases in the desert?" Rollan muttered as his horse finally caught up to theirs. Sweat beaded on his brow. *That's a good sign*, Conor thought. *At least he's still sweating. If he stops, that's when he'll be in trouble.*

"Come on, Rollan," Abeke said, rolling her eyes. "We all had a drink of water a few hours ago."

"I *know*," Rollan whined. As if in answer, Essix called out to him from high in the sky, where she was on the hunt for mice and other rodents. "Easy for you to say!" he muttered up at her.

Abeke shook her head and smiled. She looked back and forth between the two boys. "In Nilo," she said, taking something small and smooth out of her pocket, "we suck on pebbles when the water's scarce. Try it out. It'll stave off some of your thirst."

Rollan hopped off his horse, grabbed a couple of gray pebbles from the ground, then jumped back up and polished them on his tunic. He shoved them in his mouth.

"Don't *eat* them," Abeke said with a laugh. Conor sucked on a pebble and watched their antics, grateful to Rollan for bringing a smile to Abeke's face.

"Hey," Abeke called to where Kalani and Maya were trailing them. "You guys want some pebbles?"

Maya shook her head. Her fire salamander was out on her shoulder now, hiding in the shade that her hair created. Its gold-and-black-patterned scales gleamed in the sun. Maya usually kept Tini in his dormant state, but sometimes she'd let him out to feed. Tini would scamper down to the ground to hunt for a few insects and worms, then dart back to her and happily turn dormant again. Desert heat was no place for a fire salamander.

But it was Kalani who looked absolutely miserable this far from the ocean. Her shoulders were hunched, as if she'd wilted in the sun, and she rode on with a blank, downcast expression. Conor watched her closely. Unlike

Rollan, she had no sheen of sweat dotting her brow. She looked entirely parched. And listless.

"Kalani?" Rollan asked hesitantly.

"She's going to faint!" Conor shouted.

Right on cue, Kalani's head lolled to one side and she swayed in her saddle. Abeke jumped down and rushed over right as Conor called out. When Kalani started to fall, Abeke caught her. Her legs buckled, and the two girls crumpled into a heap on the ground.

Their entire procession paused. Finn came hurrying up from the rear as Conor and Rollan gathered at Kalani's side. Conor opened his canteen and poured some water into Kalani's mouth. Her eyes still looked dazed.

"Everyone take a few minutes," Finn called out, then frowned down at Kalani in concern. She took another drink of water. Suddenly the spark of life came back to her eyes, and she broke out in a sweat.

"Thanks," she said weakly to everyone gathered around her. "I'm not made for this kind of heat."

"None of us really are," Finn replied with a sigh. He squinted up at the low sun. "We should stop for the day, anyway. Sunset's approaching and we need to set up camp."

Conor looked toward the waning sun too. He felt how light his canteen was now and wondered how long they could all keep this up.

10

DESOLATE LAND

THEY TRAVELED RELENTLESSLY FOR TWO DAYS.

On the third night, Abeke slept curled on her side in one corner of her tent, while Uraza lay nearby, close enough for Abeke to keep one hand in the leopard's velvet fur. She was exhausted from the day's journey, and so very thirsty. Her parched throat kept her from falling completely asleep, and she would constantly wake up from half-conscious dreams about waterfalls and cold streams. When they first pitched their tents, Rollan had helped Finn set up a trap of pots and pans around their meager group provisions, and situated it in the center of all their tents. Abeke wished she could have a canteen of water from that pile.

Still, sleeping on the ground in the desert felt like its own form of relief, giving her a nostalgic reminder of village life.

Her thoughts wandered to Meilin. Was she still being kept in the hold in Nilo, or on one of the Conqueror ships — or had they brought her to Stetriol by now? If they ran across Conquerors soon, Abeke hoped that Meilin would be with them – even if she were commanded to fight with the enemy. Did she know about what Shane did? She must, by now. Beside Abeke, Uraza shifted closer and swished her tail, letting a low purr vibrate through her hand.

Aside from thirst, night sounds kept her constantly awake. Unlike those in Nilo, these sounds were unfamiliar to her. There were hoots and calls that she didn't recognize, yips and yowls, the slither of something scaly on the ground. Sometimes she stirred, looking around. Then she would settle back down.

Suddenly Uraza turned alert. Her head pointed toward the tent flap, and her purring changed to a low growl. Her tail swished faster. Abeke stiffened. She rolled into a quiet crouch, listening intently.

There. A scratching sound, and then footsteps. Something was outside.

"Uraza," she whispered urgently. But the leopard was already on the move – she sprang out of the tent in one bound. Abeke leaped up and followed close behind.

They charged out into the open night, completely lit by the moon.

Abeke stopped abruptly, panting, her eyes darting around the camp. She didn't see anything. Everyone still slept, and not a person was in sight. She stooped back down beside Uraza, who was still growling.

"What is it?" she whispered.

Uraza led the way. They cut a quiet path through the smattering of tents before finally reaching the center, where some of their provisions had been stacked, protected by a circle of pots and pans that were supposed to clank if anyone broke through.

But the provisions were gone.

The sacks were ripped open, their insides empty. The paper-wrapped dried meats lay strewn along the ground, and the canteens were open, some still spilling water into the dirt. Abeke gasped out loud.

"Thief!" she called out.

Immediately, Greencloaks stirred from their tents. Finn was the first beside her, while others murmured and muttered in confusion, swords drawn. "Abeke?" he exclaimed when he saw her out there. He paused at the sight of a growling Uraza. "What's going on?"

"Look," Abeke said, pointing at the ruined provisions. "Somebody took our supplies."

Finn's gaze fell on the scattered remnants. He cursed under his breath, then motioned for the others to gather. Abeke tried to temper her anger, but her own thirst made it hard for her to see all that wasted water. Who would do this? She studied the trap closely but found that nothing had tripped it.

"Huh," Rollan grunted as he and Conor came hurrying over from their tents.

They all paused when Uraza suddenly tensed and lunged for something in the darkness. The charge was followed by a piercing yelp. Abeke blinked in surprise, then found herself chasing instinctively after her spirit animal. "Uraza!" she called out.

But Uraza's attention had fixed on another creature. She chased after a blurry figure that made a mad dash in front of her, zigzagging in an attempt to shake her off its tail. Uraza pounced – this time, she caught the creature and pinned it to the ground. Another piteous series of yelps punctuated the night.

Abeke ran over to her. She arrived to see her leopard snarling at what looked like a skinny little tan-colored wolf.

Conor and Rollan came skidding to a halt beside her. So did Finn. He was the first to speak. "Well," he said. "I think we found our culprit. A dingo."

"A what?" Rollan blurted out.

"They're like wild dogs," Finn said. "But native to Stetriol."

The animal struggled in vain under Uraza's mighty paws, but she refused to let it up. The telltale signs of its thievery were on its face – crumbs of bread still dotted its muzzle. Abeke shook her head. She hadn't even bothered to check if the canteens had holes bitten in them, which they most certainly did.

"Uraza," Abeke said to the leopard. "We should let it go. It's as hungry and thirsty as we are."

Uraza reluctantly lifted her paws and let the creature scamper to its feet. It loped across the landscape for a while, then paused to look back at them. In the night, its eyes shone like two metallic discs. Then it ran off and disappeared into the shadows.

They made their way back to the provisions. The dingo had eaten almost everything. Now the only supplies they had were the small packs they'd each kept with them in their tents. It wouldn't be enough for another three days through the desert. And they were already short on water.

Abeke sank down onto her blanket. She tried not to think about the inevitable, but the thought refused to go away. If they couldn't reach Muttering Rock in the next few days, they would die out here.

The next morning, they all packed up what little they had and set out again. Abeke allowed herself a few meager sips of water. It took all of her willpower to not drink every last drop in her canteen. The desert had taken on a shimmer of light that hovered just above the dry vegetation, rippling under the sun. Sometimes, she saw things in the ripples.

The others did too.

"Are those Conquerors headed in our direction?" Maya once said, startled, her finger pointed toward the horizon.

They all paused to look. As the ground continued to shimmer, Conor finally said, "No. It's an illusion. Let's keep going."

Rollan swore he saw a giant elephant in the distance, as big as Dinesh, and wondered aloud how he'd gotten there. Twice, Abeke made the mistake of seeing a small stream babbling up ahead. It seemed like she could even hear it. But every time they neared, the stream would vanish and all they would see was more parched land.

Abeke kept her attention focused on the nearing expanse of mountains. *Just a little farther*, she thought. If they ever made it out of this desert, she would drink an entire keg of water.

The fifth day.

One of the horses perished from the harsh conditions. They all looked helplessly on when the poor creature suddenly stumbled in its steps, fell to its front knees, and collapsed onto its side with a groan. Kalani reached the horse first. But even before she could put a hand on the animal's neck, she was shaking her head. The horse shuddered, foaming at the mouth. Then, slowly, its body settled against the earth, until it used up its last breath.

They rode in silence for a long time after that. Abeke couldn't stop playing the horse's death over and over in her head.

The other horses weren't doing too well either, and the entire group had resorted to chewing on the last strips of dried jerky. Abeke traveled with Uraza in her dormant state now. The sun baked her hair and skin until they felt hot to the touch. Her canteen had already run dry. She'd sucked on so many pebbles that they no longer helped anymore. Her eyes constantly swept the shrubbery around them, searching for plants that looked like they contained water. She hadn't seen anything yet.

Wait.

As if the mere thought had given her a clue, Abeke's eyes fell on a small, nondescript plant a few yards away. It reminded her immediately of a plant she knew from back home in Nilo.

Conor saw her pause. "What is it?" he asked. He sounded half-delirious from thirst himself.

"There." Abeke pointed. "That plant."

"What about it?"

Abeke didn't answer right away. Instead, her attention stayed on the plant. It was a short, squat, ugly little thing, with swollen leaves that looked like little green sacs. Back in Nilo, they called it a water bulb, due to moisture that the plant carried in its body. This one was covered in brightly colored spiked leaves, but otherwise, it looked fairly close. She dismounted from her horse and headed over to it. Conor followed her.

"Careful," Conor said, but Abeke gave him an encouraging smile and stooped down to peer at the plant.

"I won't touch the spikes," she promised. "Look at those colors – they're probably poisonous."

She removed the knife at her belt and sliced one of the green bulbs off. She carved one end of it open. Wet, clear liquid dripped onto her hands. The others stopped in their procession to watch. Abeke stared at the liquid for a moment. It could be poisonous, of course – but at this point, she was so thirsty that she didn't care. They would all die without water, anyway. Taking a deep breath, Abeke lifted it.

She sipped the clear liquid.

Then she closed her eyes and drank deeply. *Water!* It tasted slightly sweet and wonderfully cool – before she knew it, she'd finished drinking the entire bulb. When she opened her eyes again, she noticed that the plants grew in a large cluster hidden behind dry, prickly bushes. Conor stared at her in shock. She looked back at him with a grin, and Conor's expression changed to one of delight as he realized what Abeke had found. They both turned and enthusiastically waved the others over.

"Water!" they called out in unison.

Everyone set about filling their canteens and watering their horses the best they could. The water from the plants wasn't much, but it was enough, and the mere fact that they would be able to find bulbs like this in Stetriol's barren lands gave Abeke hope that they could make it across.

"I'm going to search for more plants," she announced, then set off up the hill to find more clusters. They seemed to grow together, and if she found a few more at the base of the hills, they would be set for another week.

"Wait for us!"

Behind her, Conor and Rollan came running. Maya stayed behind to look after Kalani, who still didn't seem her best. Abeke waited until the boys caught up to her, and then the three of them set out together.

"I used to survive on bulbs like that when I went out hunting," Abeke said. "The thing is, they tend to grow in lands that have some underground water or tiny streams. If we find any more clusters of them growing, then we might be able to find a bigger water source."

"Bigger water source," Rollan said, still drinking from his refilled canteen. "Music to my ears."

They covered the short distance between the plains and the foothills. There, to Abeke's delight, they found two more clusters of the water bulbs growing. There had to be some sort of stream around. Abeke, Conor, and Rollan climbed higher up the first hill. The wind had picked up again, and the cool breeze it brought was a welcome change from the stifling heat. Abeke breathed a sigh of relief. Thank Ninani their luck was finally turning around. At this rate, they'd be prepared when they caught up to the Conquerors. Sure enough, Abeke glanced down from the hill to see the first sign of a thin, snaking stream. She laughed as they went.

"Look!"

Conor stopped so suddenly that Abeke bumped right into his back. Rollan smashed into her in turn.

"What is it?" Abeke said. Then her eyes settled on what had captured Conor's attention, and her words faded away into nothing.

From this vantage point on the hill, they could look down at a vast expanse of flatland, partly framed by the Red Mountains. The nearest side – the side they now stood on – was lined with narrow ravines. On the far side was a strange, shimmering red rock formation that plateaued high above the ground, looking like a giant ant mound.

And in the flatland's center, between all of the formations . . . were thousands of Conquerors.

ARMY

*S*O MANY OF THEM.

That was Conor's first thought.

His second: *We can't fight them. We have to go around.*

And his third: *Olvan's army should be here by now.*

"Let's go back," Conor whispered, crouching lower in the grass. All thoughts of water seemed to have escaped him. "We have to warn Finn."

"Right," Rollan whispered. He turned abruptly around and started making his way through the tall grasses. "It's a good thing we went searching for plants. We would've walked right into them. They probably have troops guarding all the passes."

"It likely also means we're close to Kovo's prison," Abeke piped up. She looked sharply at Conor. "Anything familiar to you out there? Anything from your dreams or visions?"

Conor furrowed his brows. Up ahead, the others had already quieted and turned to watch them running frantically back. Conor's persistent visions flashed through his mind – the eagle, the ape, the snake, the golden leaves. The cliff, the red earth –

"That red rock," he muttered under his breath. Then louder, "That rock formation we just saw, on the far side. I think that's Muttering Rock."

"Do you think they've freed Kovo already?" Rollan asked.

"I don't know," Conor admitted. "But we have to head there all the same. If Kovo hasn't been freed yet, it won't be long before he is."

The three charged back to the others. Finn frowned at their expressions. "What did you see out there?"

"Conquerors," Abeke said breathlessly. "A whole army of them."

"And no Olvan," Conor added, saying what Abeke had been hesitant to voice. "His forces are supposed to hold them off and give us the chance to go ahead."

"We may have arrived before him," Finn said grimly. He nodded toward the foothills from where they'd just come. "Show me."

Conor took them back to the crest, where they all got down on their bellies to watch the massive expanse of troops arrange themselves into practice formations. It seemed as if they were preparing for a big event, and Conor had no question what that event would be. Maya crawled over to join them after a while. She sucked in her breath at the sight.

"There," Abeke snapped, pointing out a lone figure standing near the front of the flanks. Her jaw clenched until Conor thought it might break. "Shane!"

Even from this distance, the Devourer's enormous

crocodile was clearly visible camped out at its human partner's side, its mighty jaws opening and closing. Conor shivered at the way its tail swept back and forth, and imagined the wide swaths it was painting in the desert sand. He looked back at Abeke to see her hands were clenched into fists. The fire of rage lit her eyes, a rare sight.

"If Shane's here," Rollan added, his own eyes sweeping the scene, "then maybe Meilin is too."

Conor's gaze settled on the strange rock formation he'd seen earlier. Something about it continued to hold his attention. *Kovo.* He called Briggan out from his passive state, and the huge wolf joined them in a small flash of light. His hackles were already up.

"Conor," Finn said, looking at the rock. "Is that . . . ?"

Conor nodded.

"We have to find a way around this army and reach the rock without drawing their attention," Finn continued. He gestured down to the formations. "I can see some of their forces down in three of the narrow ravines leading onto the plain. I'm going to assume they've taken those, as well." He pointed to two more narrow valleys that fed into the plains. "If we want to get around them, we'll need to make a wide circle east. And we'll need to do it without our horses."

Conor felt a pang at that. He looked back at the poor animals, all of whom had already been in bad shape before they set out. How would they survive in the desert?

Finn saw his face and shook his head. "We can't take them. Where we'll have to go is too steep for their legs. They will die. And if one of them startles when we're passing close to the Conquerors, they could give away our location."

Conor took a closer look at the terrain. The way he was crouched in the grass gave him a better view of the lower plains than Finn had. As he scanned the space, he noticed a tiny, shadowed path. *Paths.* In fact, there were several branches of grooves carved deep into the land, as if some ancient river and its tributaries used to exist there and had dried up decades ago.

The resulting maze of winding paths had tall walls with strange, wavelike formations and natural half tunnels. The paths carved their way all along the edge of the foothills. They stopped short of where their small troupe needed to be, but if they could pass through there completely unnoticed, they would leave behind the worst of the Conquerors.

"There," he whispered. "What if we make our way through one of those river paths?"

Finn followed his finger. His brows furrowed in thought. "It will take us dangerously close to the troops," he finally muttered. "If we're found while still there, they'll easily overwhelm us in a matter of minutes."

Conor nodded. "Definitely dangerous," he admitted. "But it's faster, and it looks like smooth, flat ground underneath those wave formations. If we pass through, the shape of it should muffle the sound of our horses' hooves, and block them from seeing the troops." He glanced at the others for their approval.

Rollan didn't even hesitate. "The faster, the better. I'm with Conor. Meilin might be down there with those troops, and we need to save her as soon as we can."

Abeke seemed more guarded. "We *are* passing awfully close," she said, more to herself than anyone else. "But if we pad our horses' hooves, we can make them travel even more quietly. Conor's right—the shadows and the formations should hide us from view."

Maya frowned. "It'll keep them from seeing us, true, but it'll also keep us from seeing *them*. We won't even have a warning of them coming until they're right on top of us. We won't have a second chance."

"I can keep Essix out," Rollan suggested. "She'll have to fly high to stay out of sight, but she can be our eyes, and if she sees the Conquerors moving toward us, she'll give us a warning cry."

"It's the best solution," Conor said, nodding toward Kalani. "We're not going to survive much longer out in these deserts, not with the state we're all in. It's time for us to take a chance, even if it's our only one."

It took him a moment to realize that everyone was looking to him as if he were the final say in the decision—as if he were now leading the charge. Conor blinked, taken momentarily off guard. Maya was right about one thing: This was their final stand. They would succeed now, or everything they'd worked toward, ever since they first drank the Nectar and joined the Greencloaks, would be for nothing. This was the final struggle for Erdas, and it fell to Conor's decision.

Memories from long ago flashed across his mind—sitting with his brothers in green pastures dotted with white sheep, standing behind Devon Trunswick and meticulously buttoning his luxurious vest. . . . How strange to be here after once being a shepherd and a servant.

He took a deep breath and willed himself to keep his head high. "I say we do it."

Finn nodded once. He didn't question Conor again. "Prepare the horses. We'll make for the path at sunset."

◄━●━►

Sunset seemed to take forever to arrive. The light turned red and purple, casting long shadows across the plains. Cooking fires began to dot the bush where the Conquerors were gathered.

The team finally made their move.

Their horses trotted slowly down the side of the rolling hills. Finn led, followed by Conor and the others, the hoods of their cloaks pulled over their heads to blend them in further with the lengthening shadows. They moved in a short, silent procession. As they went, the landscape shifted, changing from bushes and dry grasses to red, sandy rock and bare, sheer cliff sides. The walls of rock kept them safely hidden as night fell in earnest.

After a while, the mouth of the paths came into view — its walls tall and curved into a wave formation. The sound was strange here, bouncing the faint thud of hooves against the curved wall so that it came right back to them, giving it an odd echo. A cool breeze whipped their hair and hoods back.

Conor struggled to hear what might be going on beyond the rock wave, whether or not the Conquerors had followed them. The formation made it difficult for him to hear much outside of the path, though. He looked up to the sky. Essix was flying so high that in the darkness, he couldn't see her anywhere.

Behind him, Rollan whispered, "We're doing okay. The Conquerors seem like they're all cooking their suppers."

"Good," Conor replied. He could use a little bit of supper himself, but he quickly banished the thought. As if in response, his stomach rumbled. Even that sound echoed inside the wave formation, bouncing back and forth between the high bluffs.

The darker the night became, the harder it was for them to make out where they were going. The path had started to branch too, forcing them to concentrate on following the rightmost course so that they didn't accidentally lose each other. Conor couldn't see the moon tonight. Soon they were traveling in almost total darkness, their horses picking their way carefully through the terrain.

Finn kept them at as fast of a pace as he could, but they moved slower than Conor had predicted. The idea of Conquerors being right over the top of the wave formation — that at any moment, one might wander close by and look down to see them passing through — made Conor urge his horse on.

The other thing he didn't plan on, aside from the strange echoes: the wind. The shape of the narrow path channeled the air in such a way that a constant blast of cold wind beat against them, whipping their cloaks out behind them in dark streams. Conor gritted his teeth against it. After traveling through dry heat for the entire day, the sudden shift threw him off. At least it made a whistling noise as it went, muting their hoofbeats.

"How far along are we?" Abeke hissed from ahead. "It feels like we've been stuck in here for hours."

Conor tried to gauge how much distance they'd covered, but it was hard in the winding darkness. He looked over his shoulder at Rollan. "Can Essix give you any hints?"

Rollan started to answer, but a sound stopped them all abruptly.

It was the sound of hooves against dirt, but not any of theirs. They fell into a tense silence – Conor strained to hear if it came from the Conquerors' camps. But the noise had disappeared.

Then it was back again, even louder. This time, Conor could tell it came from the path far ahead that curved around a bend. A moment later, he saw the flood of light from a lantern wrapping around the path.

The rock formation bent sound so oddly that they hadn't heard the approaching party. Kalani, riding near the front, only had time to draw her sword before the other party came clearly into view.

Meilin appeared first, her hand clutching the lantern, with Jhi right beside her. An entire troop of Conqueror soldiers followed. She stared straight at them, her eyes anguished.

"Found you," she said.

12

FRIENDS AND ENEMIES

ROLLAN DIDN'T KNOW WHAT TO THINK AT THE SIGHT OF her. He didn't know how to react. He didn't know why his first thought was of the last time he'd seen her, running away from them with Abeke in tow, her mind and body no longer under her own control. He had no idea what expression must be on his face.

"Meilin," Rollan found himself calling out.

She winced at his voice but held firm. Her eyes turned yellow, and her pupils dilated to an unnatural size. "Seize them," she commanded.

The Conquerors charged at Finn and the Greencloaks. Conor called Briggan out in a blaze of light, and Uraza came roaring out of passive state to attack the enemy soldiers. Rollan called out for Essix, who let out a cry in return as she swooped down—and then he swung from his saddle and started shoving his way toward Meilin.

She didn't look like herself anymore. Dark circles rimmed the skin below her eyes, and her hair swung limply with each move of her head. But one thing stayed the same—she moved in an elegant blur of motion, a whirlwind of attacks that he was all too familiar with, taking down a Greencloak with a fierce kick at his head. Beside her, Jhi reluctantly ambled at her side, protecting her as she went.

"Take them prisoner!" Meilin shouted.

Rollan noticed that Shane stood at the very back of the patrol, a dark smile on his face.

Shane called for his crocodile. The enormous creature emerged, tail thrashing, blocking off the entire path with its size. Rollan touched the talisman buried against his chest. If the Conquerors got hold of his and Abeke's talismans, they were doomed.

Essix dove into the fray with talons outstretched, her cry furious. She lunged for the Devourer's crocodile first, but her sharp claws clicked harmlessly against tough scales. The crocodile snapped its head around, jaws seeking feathers. The gyrfalcon darted out of reach at the last instant. The beast's teeth barely missed her.

Abeke and Kalani moved at the same time, with Uraza charging ahead of them. They attacked a Conqueror and knocked him hard to the ground. Uraza pounced up onto the back of another Conqueror's horse with one huge leap, and the soldier fell off his mount with a shriek.

Nearby, Conor and Briggan aimed for Shane's crocodile, Briggan snarling and trying to find a way around its snapping jaws, to hold the animal off from the others.

"Meilin!" Rollan shouted as loudly as he could.

Meilin paused for a moment in the midst of the fighting; her head snapped in his direction. There—he could see a spark of recognition in her eyes, something within that fought to break free of the cloud that blanketed her face. He ducked under a Conqueror's swinging sword and sprinted in her direction. If he could just reach her, if he could just *touch her hand*, he *knew* he could help her overcome the Bile. If he just—

"Fall back!" Finn shouted from the fray. Rollan's attention broke for an instant. The elder Greencloak pointed at the path behind them. "The way we came!"

The Greencloaks began to break formation, turning their shrieking horses around and urging them in the opposite direction. Rollan cast another desperate look toward Meilin. She met his gaze for a brief moment. *No. I have to reach her!* Again he started to push through the soldiers, but the Greencloaks were all retreating. Abeke grabbed his arm as she passed him.

"We have to run!" she shouted.

"But—"

Rollan looked again and Meilin was lost from sight within the Conquerors. The enemy charged forward, weapons brandished. Gritting his teeth, Rollan followed Abeke and ran with the others.

Dust flew up from the footsteps and hooves, clouding the entire narrow path with a haze lit by the light of their lanterns. The dust lined Rollan's throat. He choked and coughed. His boot caught on the edge of a sharp rock—he stumbled, then fell hard to the ground.

Immediately he started staggering to his feet again, but he looked up and found himself staring straight into Meilin's haunted face.

She looked like she was about to attack him. Rollan braced himself.

Then, without warning, she grabbed his shirt collar and pulled him close. The colors in her eyes shifted abruptly, flashing from sickly gold back into a humanlike darkness, her pupils contracting. "The next fork will have no patrols," she hissed. "It'll lead you to the surface. Go!" She released him.

Rollan gaped, but he had no time to respond—or to grab Meilin's hand and pull her with him. She lost the battle in her eyes. Her pupils dilated back into big black halos, and her irises gleamed yellow once more. With Jhi at her side, she waved the Conquerors forward. Shane smirked in approval.

Rollan had no idea whether Gerathon heard Meilin's warning to him, or how it even happened, but he knew they couldn't stay on their current path for long. He turned and ran to where Abeke was dashing back to him.

"Take the next path!" he gasped at her, gesturing for her to pass it along. Abeke didn't hesitate. She shouted it up the chain, and the words traveled to the rest of the Greencloaks.

She helped us, Rollan thought feverishly as they ran. But she was still under the Bile's influence. Somehow, her willpower must be finding a way to break through the overwhelming control—and if that was the case, then surely there would be a way to save her. Rollan forced himself to keep going, instead of turning around and finding Meilin again. Getting captured wouldn't help anybody right now.

They reached the branch with the Conquerors right at their heels. Somewhere above the walls and along the plains, Rollan thought he could hear the sound of battle—

the clang of sword meeting sword, horses' thundering hooves, shouts of men. Had the other Conquerors already been alerted? If the entire army knew where they were now, they would have no hope of getting through in time. As they ran, Rollan noticed the ground gradually starting to slope up. He ran faster.

"Essix!" he shouted as he went. Overhead, his gyrfalcon's familiar cry answered. He took a deep breath, then glimpsed through her eyes. An image flashed before him — the plains from the night sky, dotted with hundreds of fires. Conquerors moving in chaotic clusters. They looked like they were fighting. Rollan peered closer through Essix's vision.

Right as their path led them up to the surface of the plains, Rollan realized that the Conquerors' army was fighting . . . Greencloaks.

Olvan and his forces had finally arrived!

Rollan blinked, returning to his own view, then looked on in awe as they all ran. Familiar cloaks flashed in the darkness, clashing with the Conquerors' dark armor, their silhouettes outlined sharply by the fires. Olvan's moose reared somewhere in the fray, his enormous antlers glinting in the dark. There! Was that . . . a soldier wearing the crest of Lord MacDonnell on his armor? And there — Rollan thought he saw Lishay, the Greencloak who had fought alongside them in Zhong, and at her side was her late brother's black tiger, loyal to her almost like her own spirit animal had once been. Rollan wanted to shout with relief. They were all here! Even a few Niloan warriors darted through the melee, their war cries joining the sounds of battle. They must have joined Olvan's forces! He wondered if Abeke's father was among them.

Then a figure flashed through the darkness that erased Rollan's smile. Zerif. He caught sight of Rollan, and the corners of his lips turned up into an oily sneer. The Iron Boar was looped around his neck—even as Greencloaks on horseback tried to shoot him down with arrows, their weapons bounced harmlessly off of him. With a snarl, Zerif turned in his saddle as a Greencloak rode up beside him. Rollan looked on in horror as he slashed at the Greencloak with his sword. The Greencloak clutched his chest and fell from his horse with a sickening thud.

Another Greencloak galloped over to Rollan. He had several horses with him, stallions that looked much stronger than the mounts they'd been traveling with. It took Rollan a moment to realize that the Greencloak was Monte, with his raccoon spirit animal perched in front of him on the saddle. The raccoon's hackles stood on end, and it hissed in the direction of the battle.

"Go as fast as you can!" he shouted as he flung the reins toward Rollan. "We'll cover you!" Then he waved reinforcements over and turned them onto the Conquerors on their tail.

Rollan let out a bark of laughter. Perhaps the tide had turned! He grabbed the reins and tried to swing up onto the horse's back. "Stop!" Rollan shouted at the horse. It only slowed slightly for him.

"Here, let me!" Abeke shouted beside him. She made a running leap, grabbed the horse's mane, and swung up in one fluid move. Then she pulled the horse to a halt so that Rollan could climb up behind her.

Ahead of them, the large red rock formation loomed close in the night. They could make it.

Then Rollan heard a familiar voice next to them.

"Poor little boy. Shall I force you to fight the girl you care for?"

Meilin materialized out of the chaos, riding alongside on her own stallion. Her hair streamed out behind her. At her back rode other Conquerors. When she glanced at Rollan and Abeke, her expression looked stone-cold. Her eyes flashed like mirrors in the darkness. Hearing Gerathon's words in Meilin's voice sent a chill down Rollan's spine. He narrowed his eyes at her.

"I'll fight *you*," Rollan snapped back. "And I'll make you pay for what you've done to Meilin."

Ahead, another patrol of Conquerors had blocked their path, forcing Finn to pull to a halt. Abeke turned their horse to face Meilin. Uraza growled at Jhi, who stayed firmly by Meilin's side.

"Meilin, it's us!" Abeke shouted. "Look—I'm okay, I made it here with the Greencloaks! Come with us!"

"She's no longer your concern," Shane called back, emerging from the shadows behind Meilin to face Rollan and Abeke. Several talismans hung from his belt, clacking together against his hip. Shane wore one around his neck, though Rollan couldn't make out which.

Abeke fell silent. Rollan looked on in rage.

Shane stared at Abeke for a moment, his brows furrowed, as if he wanted to say something. Then he seemed to change his mind. He nodded at Meilin. "I say it's time to take their remaining talismans. Don't you?"

Meilin narrowed her yellow eyes, then kicked her stallion forward. "Attack!" she said. She charged at them, aiming for Abeke and Rollan.

Abeke spurred their stallion on. The two horses charged at each other. As they drew near, Meilin hopped nimbly onto her steed's back—then, as soon as they were close enough, she jumped. She knocked Abeke right off the horse, leaving only Rollan astride it. The two landed on the ground with a shower of dust.

Rollan swung down from the stallion and rushed to where Meilin was striking out ferociously at Abeke. Abeke put her arms up desperately over her face, trying to shield herself from the onslaught, but Meilin still caught her now and then, her movements a blur of motion. Head, side, jaw, arm. She struck everywhere, far too fast for Abeke to deflect. Nearby, Uraza snarled and growled at Jhi, who kept her at bay with her enormous, deadly paws.

"Meilin!" Abeke shouted. "Stop! I don't want to fight you!" She struggled to defend herself without attacking back, but Meilin bared her teeth and continued on. Abeke's breaths came in ragged gasps, then sobs. "I *can't* fight you!" she cried out. Meilin caught her in a blow to the stomach, and Abeke doubled over in agony, all the wind knocked out of her. She wheezed.

Uraza roared in fury. She tried again to lunge toward Meilin, but Jhi muscled her way between them, baring her teeth at the leopard. Essix cried out from somewhere above Rollan. She dove at Jhi, claws extended, but seemed unwilling to inflict real damage, avoiding the panda's eyes and going instead for the thick fur of her neck.

Rollan lunged forward as Meilin raised her fist to knock Abeke unconscious. He grabbed her shoulders from behind. "Meilin—" he began.

Meilin whirled on him, knocking him right off his feet. He landed with a thud onto his back. Immediately he put his arms up to protect his head, but Meilin kicked him hard with her shin. The blow crushed his own arm against his face. Rollan rolled away, then scrambled to his feet. His arm throbbed with pain, as if just hit with a mace. His heart pounded wildly. She could kill him here, if she wanted to. She wouldn't even have to try.

"I saw you fighting it earlier," he said. "You can do it again!"

Though Meilin's face was the picture of anger, when she spoke, her voice cracked with anguish. "Leave me behind," she sobbed. "Run!" She lunged for him again.

Abeke scrambled up and tried to grab her arms, but Meilin was on her in a flash, kicking her squarely in the chest and knocking her down again. This time, Shane joined in—he shouted a command at his crocodile, and the giant creature snapped its jaws at Abeke. For a second, Rollan lost sight of Abeke behind the crocodile's towering figure. Then he saw her jump backward and whirl on her old friend with a determined stance. Beside her, Uraza let out a roar. She grabbed her bow off her back and pointed an arrow at him.

Rollan tried to remember his combat lessons, but facing Meilin, he couldn't seem to fight at all. He sidestepped Meilin's next attack, but she drifted with him, kicking out at his legs in a quick flourish. Rollan stumbled forward—he caught himself before spilling over and then dodged Meilin's short sword by a mere inch. She whirled. He could barely see her through the speed of her movements.

"I'm not leaving you!" Rollan shouted as he desperately tried to match each of her punches. One landed hard on his shoulder. He cried out in pain—it felt like someone striking him with a hammer. Meilin's eyes flashed from yellow to brown and the huge dilated pupils shrank to a normal size, then back again – whatever toll it took on her to resist killing him, he couldn't guess. *How do I snap her out of it? How do I help?*

"Such a weakling," Meilin snapped at him. Gerathon's words. "What does she see in a street urchin like you?"

"Meilin!" he yelled as she stabbed out with her sword again. The blade nicked his arm, and he felt hot blood well up against his skin before he felt the pain. "Do you remember when I first met you? Remember how much we irritated each other? Do you remember how many times you saved me?"

"Why should she remember anything about you?" Meilin hissed back. The words dripped with dark amusement. "You are nothing."

Meilin lunged for him, and the tip of her sword looked like a pointed star as it thrust straight toward his eye. Rollan ducked, stumbling, but continued stubbornly on. "Remember my fever rash in Zhong? How you stayed with me when I caught the Sunset Death? Or that time we were journeying to Samis, when you stopped that thief before he could stab me?"

Something flickered on Meilin's face – the old Meilin, the one he knew and cared about. Her yellow eyes filled with tears, but still she continued to advance.

Nearby, Rollan heard a sword clash with something wooden. It was Abeke's bow against Shane's blade. Abeke shrieked – but whether it was in pain or anger, Rollan couldn't tell.

"Remember when you fought off the sharks in Oceanus?" he said. "Do you know how worried I was?

How . . . how impressed?" His last few words wavered and his eyes burned as the memory of their last journey together hit him. Meilin let out a harsh battle cry and leaped for him, as if to make him stop. He tried dodging her again, but she caught him this time with her fist and sent him tumbling backward. The impact knocked the breath out of him—for a moment he struggled just to inhale. Meilin lifted her sword over her head. Her yellow eyes flashed wildly.

"Don't you prefer to die like this?" Gerathon's taunting words. "By her hands?"

Rollan told himself to ignore it. "Do you remember Abeke? Conor?" he gasped. Then he suddenly dropped his hands. Meilin had a clear shot at him, but he didn't bother to defend himself anymore. *I have to do this.* "You're a *Greencloak*, Meilin! You're one of us, and we'll stand at your side until the very end. You're our friend."

The blade trembled. Rollan shut his eyes and braced himself. His hands clutched tightly against the talisman on his chest. "You belong with us," he said weakly.

The blow didn't come. Rollan waited. The sounds of battle roared all around him. Then he opened his eyes carefully.

Meilin stayed suspended over him, but she had put down her blade and now both of her arms hung at her sides. Behind them, Shane glanced over from where he fought with Abeke. His face was incredulous. "What are you waiting for, Gerathon?" he snapped at Meilin. "Get the Coral Octopus!"

Rollan kept his eyes fixed on Meilin's.

Her eyes were brown—a beautiful, human brown.

His lips tilted into a lopsided smile. "If you're not here, who am I going to tease all the time?"

A laugh emerged from Meilin's throat—sad, amused, relieved. She still looked like she was struggling, but she helped Rollan stand up and then glanced frantically around the battlefield. "Keep me shackled," she said. "Don't let me go."

"I won't," Rollan replied.

Meilin called Jhi into her dormant state. The panda disappeared in a flash. Rollan seized the moment to hurriedly wrap Meilin's hands tightly behind her back.

Shane saw what was happening. His face twisted first in confusion, then in rage. He turned to Meilin. "Gerathon!" he shouted. "What are you doing? Command her to attack them!"

But Meilin's eyes didn't change. They stayed dark.

"Gerathon!" Shane shouted, angrier this time. He viciously shoved Abeke aside and hurried toward them.

"This is no time to play around," Shane snapped at her, drawing his sword. He paused in his steps when he saw Rollan take a firm stance in front of Meilin. Abeke pushed herself back up on her feet and joined him. She turned her fierce eyes onto Shane.

"If you're so worried," Abeke said through clenched teeth, "then come attack us *yourself*!"

Shane narrowed his eyes at her. He hoisted his blade higher. "So be it," he shouted. "If the Great Serpent is too weak to control a girl!"

Suddenly Shane froze in place. His eyes widened. He winced, then clutched his head as if something had stabbed him there. A terrible gasp escaped from his lips.

He shrieked once. Rollan watched as the Devourer's eyes changed . . . into sickly gold. His pupils dilated until they nearly filled up his irises.

So. It was true, then. Shane had drunk the Bile – and now, *he* had become Gerathon's puppet.

Shane shuddered violently. Then, he lifted his head and looked at Abeke again with his new eyes. He smiled and hoisted his saber again.

"I'll be ordered around by no human," he spat.

Then he touched the talisman looped around his neck and roared. *The Golden Lion!* Rollan realized too late.

The noise echoed across the battlefield – a deafening blast that knocked them off their feet.

Shane mounted his own stallion again, then called his crocodile into its dormant state. Rollan's eyes darted up, following Shane's path.

Zerif waited several dozen yards away. Wrapped around his hands were the other talismans. "To Muttering Rock!" the man shouted. Shane kicked his horse, spurring it on. The two galloped in the direction of the red rock formation.

"Quickly!" Rollan shouted, pulling Meilin over toward their horse. Abeke struggled up from where she was and ran for her horse too. All around the plains, Olvan's Greencloaks had mounted a successful attack. Conquerors were breaking into smaller, chaotic clusters, herded into position by determined Greencloaks. Far in the middle of the plain, Rollan thought he saw Olvan in the melee.

Conor came dashing up to them on his horse. He pulled to a halt and Briggan loped up beside him, his gray fur lustrous in the firelight. Conor looked from Meilin to

Rollan. His eyes were very wide, almost wild like his wolf's.

"Is she –?" Conor started to say.

"She's fine," Rollan huffed, out of breath.

Meilin screamed. Her dark irises flickered to yellow, and she struggled against her bonds.

"She *will* be fine," Rollan clarified. "She's holding off the Bile as well as she can."

"Let's get her on a horse," Conor said. "We have to go after Shane and Zerif – *now*. They're going to free Kovo!"

MUTTERING ROCK

CONOR URGED HIS STALLION FORWARD, IN THE DIRECTION that Shane and Zerif had gone—toward Muttering Rock. The vision and dreams he'd been experiencing for days now came rushing back to him: the bloodred stone, Shane astride the eagle, Kovo roaring outside his prison. Tellun's voice, ringing in his ears.

It is the end of an era. We need you here.

They would find Tellun tonight. Conor was sure of it.

Conor spurred his horse into a sprint. The others followed closely behind him. As the battle between the Conquerors and the Greencloaks raged on, Conor kept his focus on the enormous rock formation that loomed nearer and nearer. Ahead, Shane's and Zerif's horses kicked up a cloud of dust. They would reach the bottom of the rock before long. Conor clenched his jaw and urged his horse to go faster.

They reached the wall right as Shane and Zerif began to scale it. They went at a frightening pace, aided by the stolen talismans—Shane crawled across the rock as if he were a squirrel, his grip steady and sure, and Zerif was yanked up after him, sliding from foothold to foothold in a rush, tied to Shane with a length of rope. Conor swung off his horse at the foot of the rock and hurried over to the others as they dismounted. He and Abeke helped Rollan get Meilin off the horse.

All four stared up at the looming wall of rock. It seemed unscalable.

"The Granite Ram," Conor said, pointing to the talisman looped around Abeke's neck.

Abeke handed it over. "Go," she said. "We'll follow as far as we can." She tilted her head at Rollan. "Essix can send it back when you're up."

As Conor tugged the talisman over his head, Rollan turned and looked at Meilin. "Can you climb?"

"No," Meilin said immediately.

"Yes, you can," Rollan pressed.

Meilin's voice sounded frantic. "Absolutely not. I'll only be a danger to you up there. I—"

Before Conor even realized that Rollan had his dagger in hand, he'd slashed it down, cutting the rope that bound Meilin's hands in one swift movement. The coils fell to the ground in a heap, leaving her unrestrained.

Meilin looked down at her hands in horror and wonder, opening and closing her fingers.

"Rollan . . ." Conor said. "Are you sure about this? Gerathon could turn her against us at any moment."

"I said I'm not leaving her," Rollan muttered, sheathing the dagger. Meilin's eyes darted from her hands up to him. He shook his head at her. "And I'm not."

"You should," Meilin said again, although this time she said it weakly.

"No." Rollan's eyes were steady, unafraid. "I trust you."

"We all do," Abeke said. She stepped forward and squeezed Meilin's pale hands with her own. Tears started to well up in Meilin's eyes.

Conor thought back to when he had betrayed the others, and how they'd forgiven him. How, no matter what, they had to set their fears aside sometimes and put their faith in each other. He reached out and touched Meilin's shoulder. He smiled at her. "Come on, Meilin. Let's go."

Meilin shut her eyes and her tears overflowed, spilling down her cheeks. "Okay," she whispered. "Thank you." She looked at each of them in turn. "For everything. I'll fight Gerathon with everything I have. I promise."

Conor glanced up the rock. "I have to go."

"Be swift," Abeke said. "We'll be right behind you."

Conor clutched the talisman tightly. Suddenly it felt as if he could see every single foothold on the entire sheer rock side. He gave a mighty leap. The Granite Ram shot him up into the air — he landed instinctively in a spot where he could find footholds. "Hold on!" he called down to the others. Then he took another wild leap to another hold. Wind rushed past him. When Conor chanced a look down, a prickly sensation rushed up his spine. He had covered over fifty feet in the span of a few seconds. The others followed his path at a slower rate while he jumped ahead. He glanced up to where Shane and Zerif dashed. Then he leaped again.

A piercing cry rang out overhead. For an instant, Conor flinched and thought he would see Halawir flying overhead, just like in his nightmares. But the cry came from Essix. The gyrfalcon flew ahead of them, calling out a shrill warning. Conor looked up to see Shane wielding the Crystal Polar Bear. His eyes widened.

"Watch out!" Conor yelled down to the others. As he said it, a violent explosion shook the cliff side – followed by the sound of crumbling boulders. Shane had knocked an avalanche of debris down toward them. Essix shrieked and darted away from the cliff. Conor made a giant leap out of the rocks' way. An enormous boulder hurtled past him, hit the edge of the sheer wall, and crumbled into smaller rocks. They barely missed Abeke, who managed to fling herself to one side.

More rocks came tumbling down. Conor leaped from side to side as Shane struck out repeatedly with the Crystal Polar Bear's invisible arms, raining more debris onto them. "Spread out!" Conor shouted down to the others. He saw Abeke taking the lead and guiding them farther out to the right. More boulders hurtled down the side, smashing entire chunks out of the wall and adding to the avalanche.

I have to distract Shane. Conor jumped and climbed to the opposite side of the wall, forcing Shane to concentrate on stopping him. He coughed from the dust stirred up by the falling boulders. Halfway there, Conor took another flying leap, and then another, moving as fast as he could. But Shane and Zerif had the Marble Swan. With the extra burst of agility it would give them for their climb, they would undoubtedly reach the top before he could.

The thought of Shane and Zerif releasing Kovo from his prison spurred Conor to even greater speeds. If Kovo escaped, all would be lost.

Faster. Almost to the top. Conor let out a yelp as another sudden avalanche of rocks nearly sent him toppling down. He gripped the wall precariously, his feet dangling for a moment. An image of himself plummeting to his death flashed through his mind. Conor clenched his teeth and pressed himself close to the rock wall. Thanks to the Granite Ram, he found his footing.

Shane and Zerif had already cleared the top. At least the rain of rocks had stopped. Conor spared a second to make sure the others were all still climbing, and then he made three more giant leaps. He lunged up with his arm on the last leap — and his fingers curved around the top of the cliff side.

Exhausted, he pulled himself up.

Conor yanked the Granite Ram talisman from around his neck and held it aloft to Essix. The falcon snatched it from his hand with startling quickness and carried it away to the others.

From the top of Muttering Rock, he could see the entire expanse of red and brown plains surrounding the rock formation, stretching endlessly in every direction. A faint sliver of sunlight peeked up from the eastern horizon, bloodred in color.

Conor pulled himself up to his feet. "Briggan," he gasped, calling for his spirit animal. With a flash of light, the wolf appeared at his side, already growling. Conor's gaze fell over the plateau he now stood upon.

It looked like something out of his nightmares, and yet also entirely unfamiliar. Red rock. Dead, crooked trees, so unlike the golden leaves he always saw drifting in his dreams. But what commanded his attention was an enormous stone temple standing in the center of the plateau, composed of a ring of towering pillars and twisted wood that looked distinctively like ancient, petrified antlers.

One of the pillars was carved in the shape of an elk — Tellun's image, he realized — as if standing permanent guard. Each pillar stretched high toward the sky, casting long shadows against the ground. In the temple's center, trapped behind the circle of twisting antlers, was the yawning mouth of a pit. Shane and Zerif now stood beside this pit. Conor's throat constricted.

In the waning darkness, he also made out the smooth coils of a snake, and the hulking figure of an enormous eagle. Gerathon and Halawir were here. The hackles on Briggan's back rose, and his growling grew louder. Conor searched frantically for the mighty elk too, but there was no sign of Tellun.

Conor's eyes darted to the pit. It was huge and black, an endless, yawning hole in the earth. Around the edge of the pit's mouth, Shane and Zerif had arranged all of their talismans, each spaced evenly apart. The pit looked empty.

Shane met Conor's gaze momentarily. His eyes were cold and hard — and full of triumph.

Oh, no.

Kovo had already been freed.

A dark figure crouched in front of the pit, his body illuminated by flashes of lightning. The sunrise had lightened the sky, and Conor could now make out the beast's scarlet eyes. It was an ape. A gorilla.

Kovo.

Kovo lifted his fists to his chest and pounded it twice. He vaulted onto his hind legs and roared again. Conor couldn't believe how big he was — he blocked the sun entirely. Behind Conor, the others had finally crested the cliff and looked on in shock.

Kovo smashed his arms back down to the earth, shaking the entire plateau. His mouth curved at Conor and Briggan in a slanted smile. "Ah," he said, his voice deep, angry, and ancient. "One of the Four Fallen." He glanced behind them to see Rollan, Abeke, and Meilin with their spirit animals flashing out of passive state. Essix swooped down to join Rollan. "I am glad you've returned, my brethren. I did not wish us to part on such bad terms." He glanced in disdain at the statue of Tellun behind him, then back to Conor. "I've been waiting for you to arrive."

Briggan's fangs gleamed. Conor had never seen his wolf so enraged.

Kovo laughed at Briggan's expression. Then he turned his stare back to Conor. "Thank you for answering me," the ape said.

Conor frowned. His mind swirled in confusion. "What are you talking about?" he snapped back. He glanced around the plateau again. *Tellun. Where is he? He's supposed to be here!* "Tellun!" he tried calling out.

Kovo's smile widened. "There's no use. Tellun is not here, boy."

"B-but . . ." Conor stammered. "The visions . . ."

"Tellun didn't send those visions to you," Kovo answered. "*I* did."

Kovo did. Conor's eyes widened. They had traveled all this way not by Tellun's beckoning, not to stop Kovo from escaping his prison—but because Kovo himself had called them here, deceived them into it. No wonder Conor had been able to see it even when Briggan was in his dormant state, even when he should not have been able to have such dreams. Kovo had been waiting here for them to arrive, *with the final talismans*. The realization hit Conor hard. *I should have known.*

"You . . ." Conor began. "You brought us here to get the last talismans."

Kovo chuckled once. His dark eyes glinted bloodred in the light. They locked on the Granite Ram hanging around Abeke's neck, then to the Coral Octopus around Rollan's. "Clever boy," he said. "I hadn't intended you to make it all the way up Muttering Rock. Shane failed to stop you in the plains below. Ah, well. No matter. The talismans are here."

Fooled. Deceived. Betrayed. Conor felt so helpless and ashamed.

"Don't look so disappointed," Kovo said, still smiling. He reared up onto his hind legs again. "I will put them all to good use."

Then he slammed his fists into the ground.

The blow radiated out from Kovo in a ring of dust. Conor fell flat again as the entire plateau disappeared in a haze of light. Through it all, Conor could see the talismans arranged around the pit as each begin to glow a different color. Their glow grew brighter and brighter, wider and wider, until the colors all fused into one. Conor shielded his eyes from the blinding light.

Then the light vanished.

When Conor opened his eyes, the talismans around the pit were no longer there. Instead, a beautiful staff made of what looked like radiant silver wood sat in Kovo's open palms, gleaming under the churning black clouds. The top was curled in the shape of a shepherd's crook, a silhouette that Conor knew all too well. Sparkling white lines ran down its length. Kovo took the beautiful staff and held it high over his head, then slammed it down onto the ground. The stone pillars and twisted antlers around him trembled, then cracked. He took a deep breath.

"The Staff of Cycles," he said reverently, "is *mine.*"

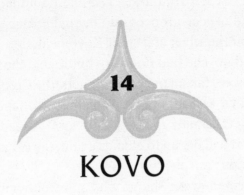

14

KOVO

KOVO HAD SENT FOR THEM. KOVO HAD TRICKED CONOR. All this effort, all they'd lost on the journey to Stetriol – the Greencloaks at the bay, the *Tellun's Pride*, Dorian – had been at the request of Kovo, who'd expected them to appear all along.

"We have to get out of here," Conor suddenly said beside Abeke. He grabbed her hand and nodded at Rollan. "They'll get our talismans."

They only managed to sprint a few steps to the edge of Muttering Rock before Halawir launched himself from his perch. He reached the edge long before they could, then spread his enormous wings, blocking out the sky. They all stumbled backward from a blast of wind. Halawir landed near the ledge, his eyes fierce and menacing.

"Where are you going?" he said in a harsh, taunting voice.

Abeke backed away from the eagle's sharp talons, then whirled around to face Kovo again. Her friends reluctantly did the same. They were trapped here. Abeke's hand tightened so hard around the Granite Ram that she could feel it digging deep grooves into her palm. Her eyes stayed focused on the silver staff that Kovo held aloft. What the staff could do, she had no idea – but it held the combined power of every talisman except for hers, the Coral Octopus, and Tellun's Platinum Elk. What would happen if the remaining talismans fused with it too? Already, the sky above them had begun to change again, the clouds rimmed with ominous purple.

A movement from Shane, who still stood with Zerif by the pit, distracted Abeke. He took several steps toward Kovo. "I've fulfilled my promise," he said. He stretched one hand out. "I brought them to you. Now, it's your turn."

A hungry light had appeared in Shane's eyes, taking over the cold triumph that Abeke had seen there moments earlier. Her hand that wasn't clutching the talisman now clenched into a tight fist. Shane was asking Kovo to hand over the staff.

Kovo cast Shane a brief look. He said nothing. Then he turned away again and nodded toward Gerathon. The serpent's tongue flicked out once, as if in agreement, and her scaly mouth curved into the semblance of a grin. The hunger on Shane's face wavered. For the first time, Abeke saw doubt there – *real* doubt.

"You're not worthy to rule," Kovo finally said, his deep voice rumbling. He didn't even bother looking at Shane. "Never speak of it again to me."

Shane's confusion changed to shock, then incredulity. Then, rage. It twisted his face and made him hideous. "You *promised* me," he snapped. "Everything I've done, all I've sacrificed." He paused in his rant to look at Gerathon.

Sudden realization hit him as he studied the serpent's cold gaze.

"You . . . !" Shane choked out, pointing at Gerathon. In the depths of his rage, Abeke could hear raw grief. "You killed Drina for *nothing*!"

Gerathon's eyes slitted as her mouth grew wide. "Not for nothing," she corrected him, looking to Zerif. "Drina believed that we served your pitiful family, when it was you who served us. You should have known, Shane, from the very beginning."

"You *coward*!" he snarled. "Forcing us to do your dirty work. You call yourself a Great Beast!"

Gerathon just laughed. "Careful, boy," she said. "Lest you value your life so little."

"*You —*"

"Do you know how painful death can be?" Gerathon hissed. Her slithering coils pushed her higher, and she stretched her neck up until she towered over them. "I can make you *scream* when you die, and this time, it *will* be for nothing." Her fangs gleamed. "Nothing but my amusement."

Shane couldn't seem to fathom what had just happened. He looked from Kovo to Gerathon, then back again, as if expecting something to change if he stared hard enough. In spite of everything, Abeke couldn't help feeling a twinge of pity for him. But the pity didn't last long, not when she thought back to what Shane had done to Meilin, to how many deaths he had been responsible for . . . to how he had made her trust him.

No. Don't. She forced her heart to harden and hate. *This is what it feels like, Shane, to be betrayed by those you trust.*

Kovo turned his attention back to the Four Fallen. He hoisted the staff again. "He who controls the Staff of Cycles," he roared, beating at his chest, "controls the Evertree. The fate of Erdas. He controls *all*." He narrowed his dark red eyes at them, focusing particularly on Abeke and Rollan. "You have lost! Give me your talismans. You have no use for them any longer, and I will put them to very good use. The world *needs* the talismans to bind together. Hand them over, kneel to me, and I promise you mercy."

"Like you *promised* Shane you would let him rule?" Rollan snapped. "You keep using that word — I don't think it means what you think it means."

Kovo's mouth curled up as he bared his teeth. "Resist," he roared, "and I will destroy you all."

For a moment, no one moved.

Then Zerif stepped forward and bent his knee to Kovo. He lowered his head. Abeke watched, stunned. An oily man to the end — how quickly he turned his back on Shane, now that it seemed all was lost.

"I pledge my loyalty," Zerif said to Kovo.

Shane let out an enraged cry. Then he called on his crocodile. It burst forth in a flash of light, front legs reared up and jaws already open — Shane grabbed one of its spikes and leaped onto its broad back. The crocodile's front legs smashed down to the ground, shaking the earth, and they lunged for Kovo.

Shane didn't even cover half the ground between himself and the ape before his crocodile suddenly halted in mid-step. Shane let out a wrenching shriek of pain. Then he fell from his crocodile's back and collapsed to the ground. He writhed. Abeke gasped.

Gerathon turned her control on Shane, forcing him back onto his feet and toward them. Abeke instinctively looked toward Meilin. As she feared, Meilin's pupils dilated and her irises faded to yellow. She shook her head violently. The color of her eyes flashed between dark and gold as she fought against Gerathon's pull. "Go!" she shouted at the others. "Don't worry about me – fight Shane and Zerif!"

"Now," Gerathon hissed. *"Attack!"*

Shane tried to resist, but Abeke could tell that his limbs moved of their own accord. He fixed his mindless stare on them and lunged.

"Go!" Conor suddenly shouted.

He, Rollan, and Abeke surged forward as one, their spirit animals at their sides. Conor and Briggan aimed for Shane and his crocodile, while Essix flew ahead of Rollan and opened her talons at Zerif. Zerif called his jackal – and for the first time, they saw the tawny animal emerge. It lunged for them with frightening speed. Shane aimed for Abeke, but Uraza leaped between them with an earthshaking roar. She attacked Shane's crocodile with claws extended.

Something black and white flashed in the corner of Abeke's eyes. Jhi! The panda reluctantly stayed at Meilin's side as Meilin struggled against her bonds, throwing herself at Abeke with all of her strength. Her eyes were completely yellow now, her pupils fully dilated. Abeke jumped backward. Even fighting against the control, Meilin was a formidable opponent. She kicked out at Abeke, trying to trip her, but Abeke managed to dodge it and throw Meilin to the ground. Meilin struggled wildly, unable to stop herself.

"I'm sorry," Abeke said breathlessly, "but I have to do this." Then she hit Meilin in the jaw, right where she knew she would knock the girl unconscious.

The hit landed where Abeke wanted it. Meilin's limbs went limp, and her eyes turned dazed. Abeke set her gently down, then leaped up and charged at Shane.

She had just reached him when Kovo lifted his staff and pointed it at all of them. A violent flash of light exploded from it, engulfing everyone.

Abeke halted. She threw her hands up to shield her face. Then, unbelievable pain stabbed her.

15

BREAKING BONDS

ROLLAN CRUMPLED TO THE GROUND WITH A CRY OF agony. His muscles felt like they were on fire. His joints cramped up. *What's happening?* His head clouded with a tight, painful tingling, and for a split second he felt as if he wasn't himself at all—that he was a complete stranger, and his real form was floating somewhere outside his body. For a moment, he was reminded of when he had been sick in Zhong. His thoughts flitted away as confusion clouded him. *Who am I?*

Nearby, he saw Uraza stumble and fall with a pained growl. Essix let out a shrill cry—her flight turned erratic. She landed with a crash, sending up a shower of dust, her wings splayed out in agony.

"Essix!" Rollan managed to shout through his own pain. He tried to crawl toward her, but another spasm of pain lanced down his legs, forcing him to curl up in a ball. Tears sprang to his eyes. Through his blurry vision, he could see that Conor and Abeke had fallen too.

Kovo roared in triumph. He stepped away from the edge of the pit, his staff still glowing in his hand, and walked toward Abeke. *He's going to take the Granite Ram*, Rollan thought. He struggled to get up, but his limbs felt weak and useless. He could only look on as Kovo towered over Abeke, effortlessly shoved the girl's arms aside, and opened his giant hand toward her. Rollan's eyes widened in horror. *He's going to crush her.*

Abeke cringed away from the enormous fingers as they reached for the talisman looped around her neck. With one vicious yank, the talisman snapped free from its rope.

"No!" Rollan managed to shout. He glanced at Essix's struggling figure again. *I have to help her!* "Essix, come here!" He pointed to the spot right above his heart. Essix turned her head toward him, her eyes full of agony. Rollan wasn't even sure that she *could* go into the dormant state after Kovo's attack—but being dormant had to be better than letting her suffer like this.

Essix let out a weak cry before vanishing in a flash of light. To Rollan's relief, she reappeared over his heart in her usual place. A small surge of energy rushed through him—for now, he felt momentarily stronger. Rollan looked toward the others.

"Use the dormant state!" he called to them.

Conor called for Briggan, and Abeke for Uraza. Each spirit animal disappeared in a flash of light. Only Meilin stayed unconscious on the ground, Jhi beside her.

Conor shook his head, as if to clear it. His expression was still contorted in pain, but the little surge of strength his spirit animal had given him allowed him to crawl up onto his knees.

Kovo lumbered to Rollan's side and loomed over him. Rollan could only hold a weak arm up in a vain attempt to stop him before he grabbed the Coral Octopus hanging around Rollan's neck and pulled it free. Rollan's heart dropped.

Kovo had all of the talismans now.

The ape lifted the staff and set its point down on the ground. He tied first the Granite Ram and then the Coral Octopus around the top of the staff, using the broken chains that had once held them in place around Rollan's and Abeke's necks. As if in response, the earth shuddered. Rollan's fingers raked through red dust, leaving long scratches. He gritted his teeth as pain continued to pour over him. There was nothing he could do.

"Thank you for your cooperation," Kovo said to them, although nothing in his sneer gave any indication that he felt grateful. He patted the staff in a taunting gesture, as if daring Rollan to come retrieve it. Then he tightened his fist around it and turned his back. "Come," he called to Halawir and Gerathon. "The Platinum Elk is all that is left."

The Platinum Elk. Rollan struggled up as Halawir took to the skies, carrying Gerathon in his talons. Kovo disappeared over the edge of Muttering Rock, leaping into what seemed like oblivion to the ground far below.

They'd gotten away.

With Kovo's departure, the skies changed color again, shifting from black and blue to an eerie, dark red.

"This is from my vision," Conor said beside him, his face turned up to the sky with a stunned expression. "This was when I saw Tellun."

But Tellun was nowhere to be seen now.

Zerif was the first to bolt. He scrambled to his feet, suddenly freed of Gerathon's control, and called his jackal back into its dormant state. He shot a quick glance at Rollan. Then he turned away and hurried to the edge of the rock. Rollan wanted to shout at him. He wished he were strong enough to give chase. But Zerif was already gone.

Conor let out a groan nearby. "Are you okay?" he asked Rollan.

Rollan gingerly stretched his limbs. The sharp pain that had crippled him seemed like it'd started to fade now. The fog that had shrouded his mind lifted too. He gradually felt more like himself again. Rollan tested his fingers and toes, then pulled himself into a crouch.

"Yeah, I think so," he replied. He got up laboriously. "What did Kovo do to us? The way my bond with Essix stretched . . ." He paused, shuddering at the memory. "It felt like my arms getting pulled out of their sockets. I thought it was going to tear me apart. Was that . . . bonding sickness?"

Conor shook his head. "I don't know. Maybe. But whatever it was, the staff must have caused it."

They both went to check on Meilin, who nodded weakly at them, her face crinkled in shame. Jhi ambled over to her and nuzzled her gently. At first, Meilin couldn't seem to bring herself to look at her panda. Only when Jhi uttered a low, mournful growl and nudged Meilin with her nose did she finally turn her eyes up. Meilin put a hand on Jhi's nose, then hugged her muzzle. Jhi stayed perfectly still. Her gesture said everything Rollan wanted to. It wasn't her fault. None of this was.

Then they turned to Abeke.

But Abeke was already up and moving, walking past them with a grim, determined gait. She was headed toward

Shane, who still lay on the ground. He'd looked so powerful while on the battlefield below – but now, after Kovo had cast him aside, he looked defeated. His eyes, flashing and furious only moments earlier, were hollow and empty. He stayed in a fetal position, his arms and legs limp.

His crocodile was gone now, back in its dormant state, and he made no effort to move. He didn't seem to care about his well-being anymore. He didn't even seem to notice Abeke approaching. Whatever spark of power that had driven him before was gone from his face, leaving behind something empty and forlorn.

At first, Rollan thought that Abeke would help him up, kindhearted even after all Shane had done to hurt them. But when she reached him, Abeke kicked him hard with her boot instead. Her heel caught him under his ribs. Shane's cry echoed out over the desert. He coughed breathlessly.

"Get up!" Abeke snapped. "I said, *get up*." Her voice sounded completely cold. Rollan didn't know what to make of it. He had always thought he would cheer the day when Abeke finally got her hands on Shane. But somehow, seeing her like this, merciless and vengeful, gave him little pleasure.

Still, it was hardly his place to say anything. So he watched silently with Conor and Meilin as Abeke forced Shane, swaying, to his feet. Behind them loomed Tellun's stone temple, as if the Great Elk himself looked down on the proceedings.

Abeke bent down and picked up Zerif's discarded sword, pointing it toward his neck. She narrowed her eyes at Shane.

"Come on," she said. "Fight me."

16

DUEL

THE LAST TIME ABEKE HAD CONFRONTED SHANE, THEY were at Greenhaven, and she'd seen him turn her kindness against her, stealing their talismans and running away like a coward. Now, as she faced him once more, all of his past betrayals came hurtling back, overwhelming her.

Shane hugging her with open arms in Samis, whispering into her hair how much he'd missed her.

Asking her to stay with him before they reached Greenhaven, claiming he wanted the others to accept him.

That twilit evening on the boat, when he'd confided in her about the loss of his sister and his fear of Gerathon . . . and he'd told Abeke she was amazing.

All were false memories – humiliating reminders of her gullibility. Shane had deceived her into caring for him, sympathizing with him, pitying him.

Lies.

Abeke's anger rose with each poisonous thought. She glared at Shane's swaying, weakened figure, and then lifted Zerif's sword with one hand. She slapped Shane in his side with the dull edge. He winced, hissing in pain through his teeth.

"I'm not going to tie you down," she said furiously, "because you are already weak. I don't need to bind an enemy who's as cowardly as you." She slapped him again with the sword. "Come on. Are you scared now? Hanging your head, now that you've been left behind?"

Shane circled her warily while the others looked on, their uncertainty clearly written on their faces. None of Abeke's friends seemed quite sure what to do. But Abeke didn't pay attention to their hesitation. She barely heard them call out her name. All she saw before her was Shane.

"Abeke," Shane said, steering clear of the range of her sword. "I'm sorry. You don't understand how hard it's been for me—"

The tragedy in his voice made Abeke's anger boil over. She screamed and lunged at him. Shane tried in vain to dodge it, but the blade of her sword glanced off his shoulder, leaving a blooming red stain. He winced and hobbled away.

"I still remember when you sparred with me for the very first time," Abeke said as she started circling again. Her hand was trembling now. "You had a pretend-assassin attack you during the match, so I'd think that it was real. I was so sure of you—even after you'd already lied to me!" The memory came back to her with stinging clarity. How ironic, she thought, that their first session was a harbinger of the betrayals to come. Abeke gritted her teeth and struck out again.

"Abeke, please!" Shane shouted as he dodged. "Listen to me!"

"Why should I?" Abeke shouted back. "You're the Devourer! You tried to kill all of us!" Her voice grew louder and louder, until it was raw with her heartbreak. "I trusted you! *I defended you! How could you?*"

"You summoned *Uraza*!" Shane suddenly spat. He sounded furious now. Abeke was almost taken aback. "Do you ever think about that? You didn't *choose* for your spirit animal to be one of the Four Fallen — you were *handed* a *hero's* choice. How easy that is for you! What about me? Do you think I had a choice?"

"You always have a choice!"

"What if you had been me?" Shane pressed on. "What if you were the crown prince of an island prison — a nation *condemned* by the Greencloaks for the crimes of their ancestors? What would *you* do?"

He's baiting you again, Abeke thought. *He's good at it.* She steeled herself against his words as she attacked again, purposely using the same move she'd used on him during their very first training session together. Her hands were shaking, despite her best efforts to steady them.

Shane stumbled backward, still talking. "I watched the bonding sickness destroy my mother and father, and turn my sister into someone I didn't recognize. Did *you* ever have to go through that? Spirit animals were a *curse* in Stetriol! The Greencloaks decided we weren't worthy of their precious Nectar. So they abandoned us without a second thought. Did they abandon *you*? Did you have *any* idea that Stetriol even existed?"

Abeke sliced at him again with her sword, catching him this time in his side. He winced and gritted his teeth. "Then my family was approached by Zerif, who brought us the secret location of Gerathon's talisman. With it came the Bile—the only cure for bonding sickness that we'd *ever* seen." His voice grew louder. "Don't you understand? I thought I was saving my people, Abeke! I truly, honestly thought—"

Abeke growled. She charged Shane with Zerif's sword pointed forward.

To her surprise, Shane paused. His tense stance suddenly relaxed, and he shook his head. "Just do it," he murmured. Then he held both of his arms out to either side, leaving himself completely open for Abeke to attack.

Abeke couldn't stop—she twisted the sword at the last moment, striking him hard in the chest with the pommel. The impact knocked him off his feet. He fell to the ground without even a cry. Abeke stood over him, breathing hard.

Shane coughed. He kept his head bowed this time, and his hair fell over his face. "I thought . . ." He trailed off for a second. "I wanted to be worthy. It's so easy for you to feel that way. You were chosen for greatness. What about the rest of us? I only wanted the same."

To Abeke's dismay, she felt her heart waver. She narrowed her eyes.

Shane finally looked up at her. "I'm sorry," he said. "I'm so sorry, Abeke. For everything. You meant so much to me—you were my only true friend. I remember everything about you ever since we first met. It killed me to have to betray you, because I didn't want to lose you. I sacrificed so much . . . my sister . . ." He winced visibly. "But I had no choice. I'm bound to the Bile, just as helplessly as your friend Meilin."

Don't. Abeke closed her eyes and pushed his words out of her head. She thought back to Shane's cold eyes, the way he had violated their trust at Greenhaven and imprisoned Meilin. All of the horrible things he'd done. How did he manage to sway her like this every time? *What's wrong with me?*

Abeke lowered her sword. The fight had suddenly gone out of her, but when she spoke again, her voice still came out cold.

"Well, I'm sorry too, because you mean nothing to *me*," Abeke said to Shane.

Shane opened his mouth to speak, but then closed it again. He stared at her for a long moment. Finally he looked away. His mouth tightened into a line.

Conor appeared with a bit of rope, and Abeke looked at him gratefully. He tied Shane's arms tightly behind his back. Shane didn't bother to struggle.

As Conor dragged Shane to his feet, the ground began to tremble again. Abeke paused, then looked to Conor, who had focused all of his attention on the shifting sky. A great wind whipped at them, pushing the clouds westward and stretching them into long dark streaks.

At first, Abeke thought that the shaking earth might be an earthquake. But as it went on, she realized that it felt less like an earthquake than it did . . . footsteps. Deep, mighty footsteps. She glanced at Shane in case he was up to something, but he seemed as startled as she was.

Conor was the one who looked toward the towering circular stone temple surrounding Kovo's prison, where a strange glow had begun to emerge from the empty recesses of the prison.

"What is it?" Abeke asked.

Conor didn't turn to look at her, but his voice sounded hushed with reverence. "He's here," he replied.

The ground shook with each thundering footstep. The sound seemed to come from everywhere at once. Abeke's eyes widened as she saw the pillars and antlers start to crumble. One pillar fell against another, toppling it, setting off a chain reaction that sent the stones crashing to the ground. The antlers, too, broke into pieces and rained down.

A blinding flash of light engulfed them for an instant. Abeke shielded her eyes with her arms. When she opened them again, something stood before the destroyed temple. Her mouth dropped.

It was an enormous elk. His fur did not look brown, as Abeke had imagined it, but instead glittered gold and silver and white. His majestic antlers branched toward the sky, and his head was lifted in a regal stance. Wind gusted all around him, but he seemed untouched by it. He walked slowly toward them. Each time his hooves hit the earth, the ground trembled.

Hanging from within the cage of his antlers shone a heavy, round talisman made from platinum, forged in the figure of an elk, its own antlers molding into the shape of the sun around it.

What captured Abeke most of all were the Great Elk's eyes—they seemed dark at first glance, but when she continued to stare, she could see red and gold, fire and earth and wind and sky, like looking into the soul of the land itself. A shudder went through her.

Tellun had arrived.

TELLUN

TELLUN WAS, BY FAR, THE LARGEST OF ALL THE GREAT Beasts. Rollan fell to his knees before the mighty elk, unable to look away. For once, he was at a loss for words.

"Tellun," Conor gasped out nearby.

The elk looked back at them in silence. Rollan could hardly bear his gaze – it was the gaze of something that had walked the earth far, far longer than Rollan ever had, that had seen the ages come and go. He swallowed hard. "Essix," he whispered, calling her out of the dormant state. *She needs to see this.* With a flash of light, Essix reappeared and flew toward the temple ruins with a cry that sounded to Rollan like surprise. Nearby, Conor and Abeke released Briggan and Uraza. Both crouched before Tellun, silent and still.

Tellun's eyes finally fell upon Meilin's figure, where she lay wincing from Abeke's earlier blow. Then he looked toward Shane. The elk bowed his head once. His antlers seemed lit from within by an ethereal fire.

Meilin and Shane let out a simultaneous gasp.

"Meilin!" Rollan shouted automatically, rushing toward her. The gasp sounded like one of terrible pain. But when he reached her, it was as if the fog that had clouded her eyes was suddenly gone.

"Meilin?" he said again, hesitantly this time.

Meilin blinked, unsure of herself. She frowned. Then she glanced at Tellun with awe. She held up her hands, studying them, and started to laugh.

"It's gone!" she exclaimed, looking at Rollan and then at the others. Her face glowed with joy.

"Gone?" Abeke said, breaking into a grin. "You mean — the Bile?"

An incredulous laugh escaped Meilin. "I think the Bile is completely gone. I don't know how I know, but . . . I can't feel it anymore!" Beside her, Jhi made a happy, grunting sound in her throat.

Rollan stared in shock. It wasn't until Tellun inclined his head toward them that he broke into a grin and let out a whoop. Conor and Abeke rushed over and wrapped Meilin in a giant hug. She threw her head back and laughed. The sound filled Rollan's heart with light — how long it'd been since he'd heard her laugh like this! He laughed along with her as they all hugged. Behind them, Tellun looked calmly on.

"I can't believe you're back," Rollan exclaimed as Meilin paused in her laughter long enough to look at him. He raised a mischievous eyebrow at her. "I've really missed making fun of you all the time."

Meilin punched his arm in mock protest. Rollan laughed, then threw his arms around her and hugged her fiercely. She hugged him back. A weight lifted off his chest, and for an instant, Rollan forgot everything they still had to accomplish. This moment, at least, was perfect.

He pulled away long enough to kiss her right on the lips.

It took him a second to realize what just happened. The two jumped away from each other. Meilin's eyes widened. Rollan flushed red from head to toe. What was he thinking? It seemed like such a natural gesture that he could barely remember what made him do it.

"I-I'm sorry," he started to stammer out. "I just—"

Then Meilin smiled. She fiddled with the sash at her waist. "I missed you too," she said, suddenly shy. She started to laugh again, and Rollan did too, running a hand bashfully through his hair. For once, he had no good joke ready. Beside them, Conor and Abeke looked on with amused expressions. Even Essix, who stayed perched on the ruins of the temple, fluffed her neck feathers up into a quizzical appearance and chirped. Jhi just looked as serene as always.

Shane stood apart from the group, head bowed silently, with his hands tied behind him. Rollan couldn't read his expression, but it was obvious that the Bile had been lifted from him too. When he thought no one was looking, he lifted his head to the sky, closed his eyes, and breathed in deeply . . . as if for the first time.

"We have to stop Kovo," Conor said as they now turned back to Tellun. "He has all of our talismans now. The only one he doesn't have is yours." At that, he nodded at the Platinum Elk. "We have no idea where he's gone."

Tellun towered over them all, his antlers catching the light. "Kovo seeks the birthplace of all life," he replied in a deep, echoing rumble.

"The . . . birthplace of all life?" Meilin asked. Her hand was entwined with Rollan's.

Tellun bowed his head once. Then he turned to look north, searching for something far beyond the horizon. "The Evertree."

The word itself sent an electric shudder through Rollan, a strange tremor, as if the very earth had spoken. "The Evertree?" Rollan whispered. Somehow, he felt it was a word meant to be whispered, something ancient and sacred.

Tellun took a single step closer to them. "When the world was very new, there existed only the sky, the water, the air, and the earth. From this new world emerged the Evertree. Some say her seed was a falling star, while others say it was forged in the mountains by the heat of the world. Her branches reached up to the heavens and her roots burrowed deep into the soil of the land. Through those roots, she breathed life into the world. The Great Beasts and our talismans were born from the Evertree. Each of us protects part of her power; it is why we guard our talismans so fiercely. The Evertree is our mother, the source of the bond between man and animal, the very soul of us – and of all living creatures. Of *you*."

Tellun paused to bow his head in reverence. A tragic note entered his voice. "You have all now felt the earth shudder – the storms in Greenhaven, the poisoning of the seas, the blizzards in Nilo. The Evertree's roots are connected deeply to the balance of life. As she trembles from the approach of darkness and destruction, so does the entire world tremble."

So that was why the world had seen such imbalance lately. Rollan tried to imagine what a life-giving tree would look like. "And Kovo is heading there now?" he asked. "What will happen once he reaches it?"

Tellun lowered his head in respect to Jhi, Briggan, Essix, and Uraza. "The Evertree was wounded during the last great war. Her soul was injured by Kovo, with a staff made of only half of our talismans. This was before the Four Fallen gave their lives to protect Erdas. She has never healed. This injury is what gave rise to the bonding sickness. Now, Kovo has another Staff of Cycles, far more complete than his last one. Even without my talisman, the staff will give him the power to call all of the Great Beasts to the Evertree. If he obtains mine as well, then the staff will give him the power to control every living being in Erdas. He will rule over all."

Kovo, ruling Erdas. Rollan shivered.

To his surprise, Tellun shook his head so that the Platinum Elk slid to hang on one of his antlers. He pointed his antlers at Conor, waiting for him to take the talisman. "I entrust you all, and the Four Fallen, with my talisman. It will be drawn to the others, just as we are being called to the Evertree by Kovo. I can feel the pull already. Should something happen to me, I want to know that the talisman lies in your grasp, not mine. Kovo's power is not something to underestimate. We must stop him now, or he will control all of us."

Conor reached out in the silence and took the talisman from Tellun's antlers. Rollan stared at it, wondering what would befall them now.

Tellun met the gazes of the Four Fallen again. "The balance among the Great Beasts has been shaken forever. There is no going back." He closed his eyes. "Our time may be coming to an end."

Conor's prophetic words came back to Rollan in a flash. *Our spirit animals may not survive this war.* The thought of ending his bond with Essix was so overwhelming that Rollan wanted to double over in pain. As Tellun's words sunk in for everyone, the sky continued to shift. Lightning streaked quietly along the horizon, warning of a distant storm, and an electric tension hung in the air. What little of the morning sun that had shone was now entirely covered by clouds.

Tellun lifted his head and sniffed the air once. "Kovo is calling," he said. "He is summoning the Great Beasts to the Evertree now."

REDEMPTION

W HEN MEILIN HAD FIRST BEEN AFFLICTED BY THE BILE, its chains had been so insidious that she didn't even know they were there, tying her to Gerathon. But now that Tellun had freed her, she felt as if she'd taken a deep breath of the freshest air. Like she had dived into a cool, crystal clear lake.

And then Rollan had kissed her. *A real kiss.*

It'd lasted barely a second, but she couldn't stop blushing and smiling, in spite of everything.

Only when Tellun said that the Great Beasts' time might be coming to an end did her smile waver. She took a step closer to her panda, and Jhi uttered a comforting grunt in the back of her throat. *Jhi.* Guilt welled up again in Meilin's chest. She had taken Jhi's presence for granted so many times — but the thought of losing her entirely, especially now that they were both freed from Gerathon's control? Meilin's heart twisted painfully.

Tellun focused on each of the Four Fallen. He narrowed his eyes. "You do not feel Kovo's pull," he finally said in his deep rumble. "Your original severance from the Evertree has made you immune to Kovo's calling." He nodded thoughtfully. "You all once gave your lives in order to save Erdas. I must now call on you to put yourselves in peril once more, to stop Kovo from succeeding."

A hush fell over them. Meilin looked on, heart in her throat. She wondered for a moment if their spirit animals would answer Tellun's plea.

Then Briggan took a step forward, his fur shining, and bowed his head before the Great Elk. Pledging his dedication. Meilin's eyes widened. *He would give his life again?*

Essix let out a piercing shriek. Jhi, too, turned to Meilin, and Meilin felt her heart lift in comfort. Jhi's eyes were warm and full of wisdom, the look of the wise earth guarding her wards, the tree offering shelter from the storm, the bonfire chasing away the cold. It was the gaze of a mother. Meilin felt tears well in her eyes. She didn't want to lose Jhi.

Only Uraza pawed the ground in disapproval, leaving grooved claw marks in the dirt. Her growl sounded suspicious and scathing, the hints of a deep bitterness apparent.

Tellun bowed his head, as if understanding. His antlers gleamed. "I apologize, Uraza," he replied, "for not standing with you all during the last war. It has always been my hope to interfere as little as possible in the natural order. But I give you my word. I will stand with you to the end."

Uraza looked wary, her violet eyes flashing. A long moment passed. Finally, she nodded once to Tellun. Then she joined the others in bowing her head.

As the Four Fallen pledged their dedication, Meilin noticed something else happening. Briggan, Essix, Jhi, and Uraza looked *larger* than usual – paws wider, legs taller, tails longer, talons sharper. They looked, in fact, closer to how they must have once been before they gave their lives. Behind each of them shimmered a ghostly aurora that resembled their former selves: towering, regal silhouettes. Meilin shivered with delight at the ghost of Jhi's Great Beast form – the gentle, round panda she knew had once looked like an enormous, fierce warrior, a hulking giant that radiated respect. The shape gleamed and glistened behind Jhi, changing colors underneath the dark sky.

In the midst of the overwhelming display, a tiny movement at the corner of Meilin's vision caught her attention. It was Shane. As Tellun spoke, Shane had stayed standing at a distance from them all, unmoving. Now he took a step toward them.

Meilin thought he might be moving to attack. "Stop!" she called out, pointing at him.

Shane stopped walking at Meilin's shout. He gave her a calm look and shook his head. If his hands weren't still tied, he likely would have lifted them in surrender. "I didn't mean to alarm you," he said. His jaw was set in a resolute gesture. "I want to come too."

"Not so fast," Abeke snapped. "This is another one of your lies."

"Yeah," Rollan added. "I don't think you're in a position to make demands, Shane."

"But what *do* we do with him?" Meilin asked, studying Shane. How strange. Not long ago, he'd seemed like such a threatening opponent. Now, he simply stood there and gave them a level look.

"I can help you," he said. "I know things that you don't."

Abeke scowled. Rollan raised an eyebrow. "Forgive us if we're a little skeptical about your intentions," he said sarcastically. Shane's expression didn't change.

Conor shook his head. "He's right. He knows more about Kovo, Gerathon, and Halawir than all of us." He took a deep breath. "I think Shane should come."

Meilin and Rollan both jerked their heads toward Conor in surprise.

"*What?*" Meilin said.

"You want him to come *with* us?" Rollan added.

"Yes," Conor repeated, his voice firm. "This is his mess in the first place. He needs to help us fix what he started."

Meilin kept her voice as reasonable as she could. "Shane is a traitor," she said. Her eyes went to Abeke, who had crossed her arms and was regarding Shane with a wary look. "Abeke, maybe you should make the call."

Abeke was quiet for a moment. Then she lifted her head higher. "I agree with Conor. Shane should come with us. Who knows what will happen if we leave him here? He might escape again. If he comes with us, at least we can keep an eye on him." She turned to Shane. Her voice became scathing. "If you're remotely genuine about anything you said to me earlier, then you'll help us track down Kovo and stop him."

Something about the thought of striking back at Kovo seemed to light a spark in Shane's eyes again. It was a small spark, a fraction of what had once burned there, but it was a light all the same. His eyes narrowed.

"I'll kill Kovo myself," he said.

Tellun stepped between them, quieting everyone. He turned his head toward Shane and held his gaze. Shane trembled as he looked into Tellun's unwavering eyes.

"Shane will come with us," Tellun finally said. "We need all the help we can muster."

Conor looked at Meilin and Rollan. "We'll be careful," he reassured them. "We'll keep him tied tightly up." He narrowed his eyes. "Don't worry. I haven't forgotten what he's done either."

Rollan sighed, but when Essix bowed her head in deference to Tellun, he threw his hands up and shrugged. "Fine. He comes with us."

Meilin looked at Abeke, who tightened her jaw and walked toward Shane. Anger bubbled in Meilin's stomach, and she told herself silently that she would still make him pay for what he'd done to her and the others.

Abeke stopped right in front of Shane. "So," she said. "You want to be worthy? Well, now's your chance."

19

THE FINAL BATTLE

THE SIDE OF MUTTERING ROCK THAT THEY HAD CLIMBED up was sheer and steep, but the opposite side sloped like a mountain, revealing a large expanse of land that ended with the white foam of the seashore. As they made their way down, Conor shot an apologetic smile at Meilin and Abeke, who still didn't look thrilled with their new companion. Shane stumbled along behind Tellun, tied to the elk with a thick length of rope. His hands were bound tightly behind him, done by Abeke and Meilin. He walked in silence, with his head down.

"Where is the Evertree?" Conor asked Tellun as he traveled beside the mighty elk.

"The Evertree grows in the place where all life began," Tellun explained. "It marks the piece of land that first emerged from the oceans."

Where all life began. Nearby, Abeke turned in interest. "Yes! We have many tales about the first land," she piped up. "Chinwe used to say that Nilo was the firstborn, birthed from the fires in the world's belly."

Tellun gave her a wise nod. "You are right, Abeke. Nilo

is the First Lands, the origin of all life." Conor saw Abeke puff up a little with pride.

"But we're in Stetriol right now," Meilin said. Rollan lifted an eyebrow at her obvious statement, but she just nudged him in the ribs.

"Yeah," Conor added. "Our ship, the *Tellun's Pride*, sank as we tried to dock in one of Stetriol's bays. How are we going to get to Nilo?"

"We will walk there," Tellun replied.

Rollan let out a grunt of disbelief. "I'm sorry," he said. "For a moment, I thought you said we were going to *walk* from Stetriol — the *island continent* — to Nilo."

"How is that possible?" Conor asked.

Tellun's antlers gleamed. "In the earliest days, when the world was very new, the oceans sat lower and left more of our lands uncovered. Conor, did your ship encounter the jagged rocks lining Stetriol's bay?"

Conor nodded.

"Those jagged teeth first existed when the oceans were low and Stetriol was young. They were called the Jaws of the Underland. The ocean swallowed them up after several millennia, but now they have returned. All of the things you have seen happening around the world — earthquakes, storms, blizzards — are turning the world back to how it looked in those early days."

Suddenly Conor understood what Tellun was saying. "In the old days, there was a way to walk from Stetriol to Nilo, wasn't there?"

Tellun paused to nod toward the ocean in the distance. "Yes. Long ago, a narrow land bridge connected northern Stetriol to southern Nilo. Now, this bridge has once again reappeared."

At that, Rollan sighed dramatically. "Oh, good to know. I wish it had reappeared a little faster, so that we could've taken *that* to Stetriol instead of nearly dying in those Jaws while sailing here."

As they traveled down from Muttering Rock and toward the ocean, Conor started to see what Tellun was talking about. Far along the horizon, waves crashed against a tiny strip of new land – it barely peeked out of the water, but even from here, Conor could see its uneven rock pushing against the sky. It connected to the Stetriol mainland.

"How far away is Nilo from here?" Conor asked. He was a bit too embarrassed to ask if he could actually walk from one continent to another.

But Tellun just blinked at him. It was strange to see a hint of mischief on such a reverent Great Beast's expression. "How would you all like a lift?" he said.

<hr />

By *a lift*, Tellun meant a ride on his back. And by *a ride on his back*, Tellun meant that each step he took made the ground below them rush by, as if they were all carried forward by some magical force.

All of them – Conor, Abeke, Meilin, Rollan, and even Shane – could fit comfortably on the Great Elk's back with plenty of room to spare. To Conor, it felt like riding on the back of a mountain – like he was close enough to touch the sky. The wind whipped against their faces as Tellun led them off of Stetriol and onto the narrow land bridge that carved a path through the ocean. Conor couldn't help throwing his head back, closing his eyes, and letting the wind comb through his hair.

The land bridge wasn't perfect. Essix, the only one of their spirit animals that stayed out of dormant state, flew ahead, shrieking warnings whenever she saw places where the rocks were still partially covered by the ocean, leaving paths as narrow as Conor was tall. The rocks here were slippery and wet. But Tellun never seemed to slow or stumble. He walked on, serene and mystical, and the earth beneath them flew past. Sometimes, the rocks sat so low in the water that they couldn't see them at all. It appeared as if they were walking on the ocean, with nothing beneath them but their own reflections mirrored back on the surface of shining glass.

As Stetriol became a thin strip along the horizon behind them, Conor's heart began to beat more rapidly. Something about the earth here pulsed with new life, like the heart of a giant creature. Conor found himself constantly searching for the first signs of Nilo.

The clouds cleared as the hours dragged into the afternoon. They traveled so quickly on Tellun's back that by the time the sun started to set, bathing the ocean in golden light, Conor saw the telltale silhouette of land rising along the horizon. He pointed at it.

"Look!" he exclaimed. "Nilo."

All of them—except Shane—let out a whoop. When Conor looked over his shoulder, he saw Abeke take a deep breath. "Home," she murmured under her breath.

The clouds had started to gather again, turning darker with each passing second as the sun dipped into the water. The wind picked up too, whipping their cloaks out behind them. Conor squinted at the approaching land. He hadn't seen this side of Nilo before—or perhaps the changing world had shifted it into something unrecognizable. The land bridge began to slope out of the water, until they were now suspended a good twenty feet above the ocean. Sheer cliffs stretched on either side of Nilo. Conor tried not to think about how high they were.

But, most noticeably, Conor could see an enormous, craterlike formation looming ahead, not far from where the land bridge connected with the mainland.

"We are drawing near," Tellun said, his low voice sending a rumble through everyone.

Fat drops of rain started to fall right as they reached Nilo. Tellun began traveling up narrow paths that winded along the crater's edge. The air was colder here, and Conor had to wrap his green cloak more tightly around his shoulders. The trees began to dwindle until they disappeared altogether, leaving nothing but low shrubs, yellow grasses, and bare rock along the path. As they climbed higher, Conor could see the land bridge winding back toward Stetriol like a slender snake through the ocean.

The sky behind them looked gray and threatening. Conor hadn't been able to make it all out from the ground, but from this higher vantage point, he could see that the clouds streaked in ominous lines from Stetriol all the way to where they were in Nilo, gathering in swirling circles over their heads. He shivered.

As they crested the top of the crater, Conor realized that it was the remnants of what must have been the most massive volcano that ever existed. His jaw dropped at the sight. Once upon a time, this volcano would have been a formidable sight, raining lava and ash on its surroundings before collapsing in on itself in a spectacular display. Now, high from his new vantage point on top of the volcano's edge, Conor looked down on the inside of the ancient, collapsed crater and saw a huge expanse of lush green land.

Tellun spoke in the silence. "You are now on sacred ground," he said. "This is the birthplace of all life. Only the Great Beasts can find this place."

The clouds overhead had turned even darker, and lightning streaked at the edges of the crater. Conor's eyes shifted to a single tree standing tall in the center of the crater. He knew immediately what he was looking at. His eyes widened.

"The Evertree." His voice came out a hoarse whisper.

It was taller than any tree Conor had ever seen in his life. It shimmered under the dark sky, glowing as if from within, a rainbow of silver and gold. Its branches reached up to the skies in an enormous canopy of shimmering leaves. Its twisting silver trunk was at least a dozen times as wide as Tellun's antlers. Pure white fruit hung from the Evertree's branches. Conor could hardly breathe as he took in the sight.

The origin of all life.

A rumble of what sounded like thunder shook the crater. They all startled at the sound. Meilin glanced back at Conor with raised eyebrows. "What was that?" she said.

"Thunder?" Rollan piped up, distracted. He couldn't take his eyes off the Evertree either.

The rumble sounded again. This time it was louder. There, standing below the Evertree's mighty branches, was a dark shape. A jolt of fear lanced through Conor. "No," he said, shaking his head. "It's Kovo's roar."

The ape lifted the staff high over his head. This time, his roar was unmistakable — it pierced the air and brought goose bumps out on Conor's arms. When he looked closer, he noticed Gerathon's serpent body coiled beside Kovo's, and Halawir perched in the branches of the Evertree. Even from this distance, they looked enormous and forbidding, more so than during their last confrontation on Muttering Rock.

But as large as they loomed, the Evertree dwarfed them all. Somehow, this gave Conor the bit of strength that he needed.

Tellun lowered his neck so that they could all slide off. Shane, still tied up, landed on the ground with an undignified roll. He grunted. Conor picked himself up and called for Briggan. With a flash of light, the wolf appeared at his side.

"What should we do?" Conor asked Tellun.

The elk kept his eyes fixed on the Evertree. "We answer Kovo's call," he replied. One of his hooves stepped forward, kicking up dust.

"We . . . answer his call?" Conor asked. He looked around at the others. None of them seemed to feel the pull of Kovo's summon.

Tellun fixed him with a steady gaze. "Come." Then he began to head down.

Meilin and Abeke called their spirit animals out too, and Essix soared over Rollan. As Tellun made his way down into the crater, the others followed, spreading out until they were all several dozen feet away from one another. Conor looked at Briggan as they walked. The wolf's blue eyes stayed locked on the Evertree and the figures of Kovo and Gerathon underneath it. His muscles were tense, and the hackles on his back were up. Conor's gaze shifted back to Tellun. They were answering Kovo's call . . . they were approaching him, right out in the open. What did Tellun have in mind?

Kovo turned to face them as they drew closer. He paused in his roar for a moment, then puffed his chest out arrogantly. Conor thought he could see a sneer spreading across the ape's face. Kovo lifted the Staff of Cycles higher, then pounded his chest with one mighty fist. He slammed the staff into the earth.

The entire land trembled at the blow. Conor stumbled, barely keeping himself from falling. The sound seemed to reverberate all across Erdas, deep into the world's core.

At first, nothing happened. Then the ground trembled again. Conor looked to the crater's horizon. What had Kovo done?

The tremors came one after another, deep and slow. *Footsteps.*

And as Conor looked on, dark silhouettes appeared all along the far edges of the crater, each spaced apart from the other, all facing in toward the Evertree and Kovo. The tremors came in rhythmic, thundering steps, like the beating of war drums. Conor began to recognize the approaching silhouettes.

Rumfuss. Suka. Dinesh. Conor exchanged a startled glance with the others as they recognized the towering shapes of the great boar, polar bear, and elephant. Arax too, and Cabaro, and Mulop, the octopus's huge tentacles sliding a wide path across the ground. A Great Swan flew beside them, her white wings expanded in a bright canopy of feathers, and Conor caught his breath at his very first sight of Ninani herself.

The Great Beasts had all arrived.

"Keep going," Tellun said in a low voice. Conor pressed his hand tightly into Briggan's neck fur, took a deep breath, and focused on the Evertree as they moved forward in step with the other Great Beasts.

As the Evertree came into better view, Conor noticed that one side of the tree had a large, dark blemish on its otherwise pristine silver trunk. The blemish was twice as big as he was, a region of black, rotting wood that seemed to be slowly eating away at everything surrounding it. An indescribable sadness sank into Conor's chest at the sight. So, this was the consequence of Kovo trying to control the tree with a partial staff. Even though it had happened long ago, the wound still looked fresh and festering.

Closer and closer came the Four Fallen and the other Great Beasts. Now their footsteps were so strong that Conor could barely keep his balance with each thundering reverberation. He had never seen all of the beasts together in one setting — dusk extended their shadows into long, endless streaks across the land, and the approaching darkness cut their enormous figures into shades of stark black and white, making them look even bigger than they were.

Keep moving, Conor reminded himself. Briggan, Uraza, and Jhi strode steadily onward, their focus unbroken. *Maybe Tellun was wrong.* What if they were feeling Kovo's summon too?

Finally each Great Beast stopped a short distance away from the Evertree, forming a ring around where Kovo, Gerathon, and Halawir had gathered beneath its canopy. Tellun halted too. Conor stood between him and Briggan, his hand still buried in the wolf's fur. His breath came in shallow gasps. Without the tremor of footsteps, the plains fell eerily quiet, the silence punctured only by the crackle of lightning and rumbles of thunder overhead. An icy wind whipped around them. None of the Great Beasts uttered a word. They stood frozen, the ominous totems of an endgame.

Kovo moved first. He pivoted where he stood, staring at each of his brethren in turn. His stare stopped on Tellun. Under the dark sky, the ape's eyes flashed scarlet. His gaze shifted hungrily to the talisman that hung from Conor's neck. The final piece of the puzzle.

"The era of our power is coming to an end," Kovo finally shouted. The wind carried his words across the plain. "The world is in upheaval. You have all seen it. I have seen it. Once, long ago, we stood against each other and let mankind destroy what should have been ours by right—the control of this world. We allowed four of our own to perish." Briggan tensed beside Conor, and nearby, Uraza uttered a low growl. Conor's jaw tightened too. Kovo and Gerathon had been the ones responsible for the Four Fallen's deaths, after all. "Now, the end of this old era has come to pass. That is why I have summoned us all here today for a Grand Council."

He paused to hoist the Staff of Cycles again. He looked up at the Evertree's gleaming branches. "But know this!" he said, pointing the staff at each of the beasts. "With the end of this era, we can begin another. A *better* era. An era where we are truly *great* again. Everything I have done— *everything*—has been with the goal of bringing us all to our former glory. When I rule Erdas, I will ensure that all will bow to us. Our power will be unsurpassed. We should not war against each other. We should unite. Join me in this. We will be true Great Beasts!"

Conor listened in silence. His eyes wandered to the others. None of the Great Beasts made a move or a sound. *No*, Conor thought desperately. *They're listening to Kovo.*

Kovo turned back to Tellun. He brought himself up to his full height, then nodded once at the elk. "Stand with me, Tellun!" the ape roared. "You once imprisoned me, but I am now free. Don't you see how much power is here for us to take?" He stretched out one huge palm. His eyes narrowed at Tellun's talisman. "Give me the Platinum Elk," he commanded. "You know what a complete Staff of Cycles can mean for us. You know you must do this, for all of Erdas. For the Great Beasts."

For a long moment, Kovo and Tellun just stared at one another. Conor's heart began to pound. *What are you waiting for?* he thought fiercely at the Great Elk, wishing he could hear him.

Then, to Conor's shock, Tellun lowered his head. "What—" Conor stammered, not knowing what to say next. Tellun didn't reply. Instead, he let his antlers touch Conor's chest, right where the Platinum Elk talisman now hung.

Kovo's eyes widened, and a slow smile started to spread across his face. Tellun was going to take back the talisman and give it to him!

"No!" Conor shouted. He couldn't let this happen. The Platinum Elk was the only thing left that Kovo didn't have. With this, all would be lost. Conor's eyes shot to Tellun's, and he put his hand on Tellun's lowered muzzle. "Please—" Conor begged. Meilin, Rollan, and Abeke looked on in horror. "Don't do it. I don't know what Kovo has done to persuade you, but you have to fight it. You—"

Tellun only met Conor's desperate gaze with his quiet one. Conor felt as if he could see straight into the Great Beast's soul. Tellun still didn't speak. The rest of Conor's plea withered away on his tongue.

Tellun lowered his head again. He made no move to take the talisman away from Conor.

Kovo's smile wavered.

"Everything lies with you now," Tellun said to Conor in a low, rumbling voice. He nodded once. "Protect it."

Conor couldn't think. He couldn't react. All he could do was clutch the Platinum Elk close and look on as Tellun turned toward Kovo. Kovo's fading smile twisted into the picture of rage. Tellun lowered his antlers again.

As Kovo opened his mouth to utter a furious roar, the Great Elk charged at the Evertree.

Blinding light exploded from the tree as Tellun struck it. An enormous force threw Conor clear off his feet. He flew backward, landing heavily in the grass. The brilliant light was everywhere—he couldn't see anything. The ground beneath him trembled violently. *An earthquake.*

Then the light vanished. Spots swam before Conor's eyes. He pushed himself up, blinking, and immediately reached out for Briggan. His hand made contact with familiar fur. As his vision cleared, Conor saw that Tellun had disappeared. All that remained was a new dark mark on the Evertree's trunk where Tellun had struck it. Conor's mouth hung open. A feeling of indescribable pain pierced him.

Tellun had never intended to give Kovo the Platinum Elk. Instead of letting Kovo have what he wanted, Tellun sacrificed himself.

Tellun had died.

Before Conor could react, he saw Rumfuss the Boar stamp the ground with his hooves. Huge clouds of dust whipped into the air. He, too, looked toward Conor and the other Four Fallen, exchanging a quiet, knowing look with them. Then he snorted loudly at Kovo.

"For . . . Erdas!" he roared. He charged at the Evertree.

"No!" Kovo managed to call, but it was too late — Rumfuss hit the tree with a force like thunder, shaking the entire crater with the impact, and vanished in a flash of light. Another dark wound appeared on the Evertree. A shower of golden leaves fell as the tree shuddered.

Dinesh, too, stepped forward and charged at the Evertree, letting out one last, enormous trumpet of his trunk before sacrificing himself. Then Cabaro the Lion let out a bone-shaking roar and charged at the Evertree too. His impact knocked Conor to his knees. When Meilin hurried over to help him up, he saw that Cabaro was gone and the Evertree had a new wound. *Even Cabaro, the vain and cowardly!* He felt a swell of sadness and kinship.

Kovo pounded his chest in rage and snarled at the other Great Beasts. "Such fools!" he shouted. "All of you! I could have handed true power back to all of us — I could have made sure we ruled together! Do you not know that our era is waning?" He roared as Suka the Polar Bear stepped forward. "Stop!" His voice had a note of anguish in it that surprised Conor.

Meilin met Conor's eyes with a wild, startled expression. "The Great Beasts are sacrificing themselves!" she shouted. "So that Kovo cannot control them! We have to help!" Beside her, Jhi pawed the ground and uttered a long, low, pandalike cry. It was the first time Conor had ever seen her in a battle pose.

This snapped Conor out of his shock. "Right!" he replied. He touched Meilin's arm and looked at Rollan and Abeke. "Briggan and I will aim for Kovo," he said. "Get Halawir and Gerathon! This is our last chance!"

The four nodded in unison. No time to waste. Conor pulled out the ax at his belt. Briggan bared his teeth at Kovo. He and Conor charged as one.

Abeke and Meilin lunged for Gerathon, with Uraza and Jhi right beside them. Rollan called Essix as Halawir prepared to take off from the Evertree's branches. They all seemed to move in a slow, blurred motion. From the corners of his eyes, Conor saw Suka change her course in mid-gallop from the Evertree to Gerathon. The Evertree's branches glimmered behind her towering shape. Conor veered to one side and crouched low as the bear charged past him. His hair whipped over his face and he turned his eyes up, mouth open, to see one of her enormous paws soar over his head. The rest of her was shadowed, a titan of a silhouette with a bright glowing eye high above the earth. Then her paw crashed down to the ground, throwing Conor onto his back. He scrambled to his feet again.

The other Great Beasts were on the move too. Arax the Ram's horns looked nearly big enough to tear the Evertree down. His hooves beat against the earth, furious and heavy, ripping up entire fields of grass as he charged ahead. Kovo tensed as the ram hurtled toward him. At the last moment, Kovo sidestepped with surprising speed. He grabbed Arax's horns and twisted hard. Their shadows engulfed Conor and everything around him. The two giants toppled to the ground with a shudder, the force strong enough to crack the earth.

Halawir took off into the air—but Mulop swung his giant tentacles up. One of them caught Halawir before he could fly higher. The giant eagle shrieked in fury as the enormous suctioned rings on the tentacle wrapped around his talons, trapping him in midair. Essix dove for him, a small, stark figure against Halawir's maelstrom of beating wings. The falcon extended her talons and hurled into Halawir with an earsplitting shriek. One of Essix's claws hooked into Halawir's left wing, throwing the eagle off balance. Halawir lunged at Essix with his gleaming, razor-sharp beak—the beak tore into Essix's wing before the gyrfalcon could pull away. Essix let out an angry cry and lunged back. Even restrained by Mulop, the beating of Halawir's wings was so strong that a funnel of wind started to form around him. The gusts bent some of the Evertree's branches, and more leaves whipped around in the air.

Conor had to fight to keep from being lifted right off his feet. As the leaves flashed past his vision, he remembered his dreams in a flash. *Golden leaves, towering tree, the Great Ape roaring.* He turned back to Kovo and gritted his teeth.

"Now, Briggan!" Conor shouted.

As Kovo shoved Arax away roughly by his horns, he turned in time to see Conor and Briggan charging straight for him. He only had time to bare his teeth before Briggan slammed into him. The wolf knocked him onto his back with a heavy thud. Briggan snapped at the ape's neck, but Kovo rolled just in time, forcing Briggan off of him and swinging a mighty fist at Briggan's snout. Briggan leaped back, narrowly avoiding the blow. For an instant, Kovo was on the ground, and his attention was turned completely away from Conor. Briggan snarled as Kovo lunged for him.

Conor made a flying leap for Kovo. His arms laced around Kovo's neck, throwing him off balance and stopping his attack. The wolf twisted around Kovo's arm. He sunk his teeth into the ape's thick wrist, making him roar in pain. Conor saw instantly that Briggan was trying to force Kovo toward the Evertree. To make him sacrifice himself in the way that Tellun, Rumfuss, and the other Great Beasts had.

Nearby, Suka let out an earthshaking roar as she faced Gerathon. The serpent had uncoiled and now towered over the polar bear, her fangs wide open.

Conor hung on for dear life as Kovo swung around, trying to shake the boy off of him. Briggan tightened his jaw. Kovo spun to crush Conor under his back, but Conor let go at the last second and scrambled away.

Near them, Halawir managed to shake Mulop off, throwing him against the tree. Blood stained one of Essix's wings, but the gyrfalcon dug her claws grimly into the eagle. Halawir looked ready to attack Essix again when a white blur of motion struck him. Ninani the Swan! Conor ducked instinctively at the sight. Wind roared against his face. Her pale wings nearly blotted out the dark sky as they beat furiously against Halawir. An angry cry emerged from her throat. Halawir, startled for an instant, forgot Essix — and the moment gave Essix the chance to strike out. Halawir screamed as the gyrfalcon's beak tore into his side.

"Conor!"

Abeke's shout shook Conor from watching the winged beasts fight. Just in time, he saw Kovo roar and throw a heavy fist at him. Conor threw a hand up in a pitiful defense. Something silver and gray blurred in front of him before Kovo's strike could land.

Briggan.

The Great Wolf struck like lightning, his fangs shooting out at Kovo's arm and locking onto his wrist before Conor could even think. Kovo's roar changed to one of pain. He swung his arm backward, taking a snarling Briggan with him, and tried in vain to throw him off. Briggan hung on grimly. The ground shook as Kovo stumbled backward. Then he lost his footing as Briggan gave his arm a ferocious shake. Kovo roared again in fury. He twisted around and sank his teeth into Briggan's shoulder.

"Briggan!" Conor screamed as he scrambled to his feet. Briggan winced in pain. He tried to continue hanging on, but Kovo's bite had taken its toll, and the wolf was forced to release the ape.

The earth shuddered. Conor glanced over to the Evertree in time to see Suka seize Gerathon's body between her thick jaws. She clamped down hard. Gerathon hissed in fury, twisting her body in an attempt to free herself, but it was too late. Suka charged at the Evertree with the serpent. They struck with the force of an avalanche. The tree shook, one of its branches snapping and crashing to the ground. Blinding light engulfed everyone.

When Conor could see again, Suka—and Gerathon—were gone. The Evertree leaned from the weight of the blow.

Nearby, Uraza leaped for Halawir, managing to grab one of his talons in her teeth, and Mulop wrapped a tentacle around the other. With the forces of Ninani and Essix keeping him from flying higher, Halawir screamed in frustration. He finally lost his balance and crashed to the ground. Arax the Ram was there, ready and waiting. He lifted Halawir with his horns, then charged at the Evertree with the eagle. Halawir tried to untangle himself, but to no avail.

Both Arax and Halawir struck the Evertree and vanished in a haze of light and thunder. Ninani and Mulop followed immediately afterward, sacrificing themselves in their wake.

Kovo threw his head back with a furious cry. "You *fools*!" he shrieked, grief mixed with his rage. He brandished the Staff of Cycles higher. "You sacrifice yourselves for nothing!" He bared his teeth at the rest of them. "Then I will destroy *everything*. I will destroy you all! I will rule Erdas alone!"

He looked down at the wounded Briggan at his feet.

No! Conor sprinted toward them. With Gerathon and Halawir gone, Rollan, Meilin, and Abeke rushed to help. Uraza pounced on Kovo right before he could lunge at Briggan again. Her claws dug into the ape's thick back hide. Kovo stumbled, giving Briggan the chance to dodge his blow. Kovo shook his body left and right – finally, with a terrifying growl, he spun so roughly that Uraza flew off of him. He reared up to his full height, pounding his chest with his fists. His eyes glowed red in the darkness.

And then, to Conor's disbelief, he heard Meilin's clear voice ring out. "Now, Jhi!" she cried.

20

THE STAFF OF CYCLES

JHI CHARGED AT KOVO. WHEN SHE REACHED HIM, SHE reared up to her full height—a formidable sight, even as a smaller version of her Great Beast self. She let out a roar. Meilin felt a sudden jolt of both fright and pride. Never had she heard such a sound before. Gentle Jhi, now a terrifying warrior. Even Kovo seemed stunned for a moment.

Meilin moved on instinct. The Bile had held her back for so long that now, to have full control over her entire body and mind, she felt completely exhilarated. She broke into a run, then stepped lightly off of Jhi's back and made a graceful, flying leap toward Kovo. Her arms hooked around his neck. He swung wildly to shake her off but Meilin kept her balance on his shoulders. She whipped off the sash tied around her waist and yanked it tightly around Kovo's eyes, blinding him. He threw his fists out around him, striking at the air. "Go, Jhi!" Meilin cried out.

Jhi lunged toward Kovo—but not before Kovo managed to throw Meilin off his back. She hit the ground hard. Stars exploded before her eyes. Kovo swung his staff at

Jhi, forcing her back, and slammed the staff into the ground again. Light burst from the crook in all directions. Meilin and her friends cried out at the brightness and threw their arms up. Meilin felt her bond with Jhi tremble, as if a string between them had just been violently plucked. Panic rushed through her. She struggled to her feet and staggered toward Jhi.

The panda looked back at her, also shaken. Uraza, Briggan, and Essix all shuddered in place – and Uraza's violet eyes flickered for an instant, turning colorless. The cobalt blue color of Briggan's brilliant eyes faded too. For a moment, it seemed as if all of their bonds would *break*.

No, they can't, Meilin cried silently. She braced herself for the worst.

Suddenly the light from the staff flickered and died. Confused, Meilin glanced at Kovo. What she saw made her mouth drop open. Another figure had lunged at Kovo, someone riding on the shoulders of an enormous crocodile. The crocodile's jaws were open, and his roar was directed at Kovo.

It was Shane.

Shane.

I must be hallucinating, Meilin thought, struggling to understand.

Shane let out a furious yell at Kovo, one full of anguish and anger. His crocodile snapped at Kovo. Its jaws clamped down on the gorilla's side. Shane slashed out at the ape's face with his saber. The blade sliced into Kovo's eyebrow, cutting deep. Kovo roared in pain. He spun sharply, yanking Shane and the crocodile with him. Meilin tried to shake the shock from her system.

Shane won't be able to hold Kovo back for long, she thought.

Then she realized that Shane was shouting something. Something at *them*. "Get him!" he yelled.

Jhi moved with terrifying speed. She lunged at Kovo with her jaws wide open. Her attack forced him backward. Meilin couldn't believe how fast Jhi was moving — this was the warrior side of her, the side that Meilin had always whined to see but that Jhi had kept hidden until the moments when she knew she had to unleash it. In that instant, Meilin felt an indescribable sense of pride in her spirit animal.

Jhi had always been the true warrior. The warrior who turned to peace and kindness first, and struck only in love and defense. The *wise* warrior. What Meilin should have wanted to be all along.

Jhi's claws raked across Kovo's chest before he could get out of the way, leaving four deep red gashes. He roared. Shane ducked the swipe, then rolled and grabbed Kovo's leg. It didn't take a huge amount of force — Shane's move was enough to trip Kovo. He fell heavily.

Nearby, Conor rose. He put his hands on Briggan's fur, as if to strengthen their connection, and Briggan managed to stagger back to his feet. Meilin marveled at how regal Conor looked. He and Briggan charged Kovo as one. Rollan and Essix did the same — Rollan sprinting forward, Essix following him in the air, ignoring her wounded wing. Abeke and Uraza charged at Kovo too. Uraza jumped for Kovo's arm, the one that brandished the staff. Her jaws closed on it. At the same time, Briggan grabbed the arm in his teeth. Together, the two yanked hard.

"Essix!" Rollan shouted. Essix dove for Kovo's face,

forcing him to throw his other hand up to defend himself. Attacked from all sides, blind and fallen, Kovo finally dropped the staff. It rolled once, until it lay at Meilin's feet.

"Now, Meilin!" Conor shouted.

Meilin bent down and seized the staff. She tossed it to Conor. Kovo let out a roar that sounded more desperate this time. But he couldn't stop Conor from taking the Platinum Elk off of his neck and looping it around the staff. Kovo's voice suddenly turned pleading.

"I could have saved you all!" he cried from where he lay on the ground. His eyes darted from one of the Four Fallen to the next, disbelieving. "If you do this, we will *all* perish! You will destroy the Evertree, and you will all die!" His gaze switched to Meilin, Rollan, Abeke, and finally Conor. "You will forever lose your spirit animals." His voice held in it a terrible tone of finality.

Conor hesitated, just for a second. Meilin swallowed hard as she met Jhi's gaze. Even in her warriorlike state, Jhi's expression was as calm and steady as ever. Meilin could feel the wisdom in her gaze, and it broke her heart. She knew what Conor had to do.

Finally Conor returned Kovo's look. "I know," he answered. His voice did not tremble at all.

Then he pressed the Platinum Elk tightly against the staff. The talisman vanished in a halo of light, and threads of bright silver lit up on the staff. It started to glow. Conor pointed it at the Evertree.

Kovo's struggles turned frantic, but the others held him firmly down. "No! You can't! *Stop!*"

Conor ignored him. He lifted the completed Staff of Cycles, took a deep breath, and rammed it into the ground.

21

THE EVERTREE

A BRILLIANT BOLT OF LIGHTNING STRUCK THE WOUNDED Evertree. Abeke ducked down and covered her ears, but the explosion tossed her easily to the ground. It shook the entire crater. Sparks of fire flew from the Evertree, quickly igniting on each of its lower branches. The giant tree groaned in agony, shuddering, and then an enormous crack split the entire tree down its middle. Abeke winced at the sight, as if the lightning had struck her instead.

Kovo let out one final, anguished cry. Then he too vanished in a flash of light and reappeared as a dark wound on the dying Evertree's side.

He was gone.

The Evertree tilted heavily to one side. Golden sap streamed from its wounds, painting trails of tears down the trunk and pooling in the dying grass around it. Overhead, the sky's dark clouds turned jet-black, swirling in spirals around the dying tree. For a moment, it seemed as if the Evertree might still stand, engulfed in flames. But then it gave a final groan, followed by an earsplitting crack. Abeke took a step back.

The Evertree fell.

It fell slowly, in the way a giant would fall, with all the weight of the world on its shoulders. Its silver and gold branches snapped, burning, and as the tree crashed to the earth in a storm of splinters, the clouds overhead finally split open with cold rain – gathered since their battle at Muttering Rock. There the tree stayed, spent, its life slowly leaking away, limbs bleeding. Abeke looked on as a torrent of rain gushed from the skies, hissing as the sheets of water hit the Evertree's furious flames. Lightning streaked across the sky in jagged rivers. Rain poured down Abeke's face.

She couldn't tell if it was rain, or tears.

From where Kovo had once lay struggling on the ground, Uraza crouched at the wounded Briggan's side. The wolf's strength was finally sapped, now that Kovo was gone. Conor had already hurried to his spirit animal, wrapping his arms around the wolf's neck. Essix landed nearby, limping, and hobbled over to join them. Jhi sat beside Briggan, her head bowed, and Meilin stood silently next to her. Slowly, Abeke walked over until she reached Uraza. She leaned down, petted Briggan, and placed her head against Uraza's chest. A deep, empty feeling weighed against her.

From over Uraza's shoulder, she noticed Shane sitting some distance away. He looked dazed, his eyes locked on the Evertree. She couldn't be sure, but his expression seemed genuinely tragic.

The colors in the sky began to change. At first, Abeke thought it was the same thing that had happened while they were at Muttering Rock – but this time, the colors were brilliant and bold, not dark and ominous. Bright scarlet and gold, green and turquoise, a rainbow of light that swirled and sparkled among the clouds. The colors blended together seamlessly, magnificently, into ribbons that trailed from the sky over them all the way to the edges of the horizon. It seemed as if the life in the Evertree had left the physical world and bled into the heavens.

Abeke could hardly bear the beauty of it.

As Abeke stared in awe, the colors began to shift into shapes and silhouettes. They solidified into a vision. Abeke's eyes widened. She gasped, and her hands tightened against Uraza's fur. The vision intensified, spreading until it covered the entire sky. She saw a beautiful golden land; a clear, breathtakingly blue ocean; a sky glittering with stars; a world young and pristine. The beginning of everything. She saw a tree sapling with silver bark and golden leaves growing from the new soil of a dying volcano. She *felt* the life that the Evertree's roots breathed into the land, the beginning of the world. She witnessed the birth of the Great Beasts that emerged from this newfound energy, and their sacred oath to watch over the world and guard it from harm. The way things used to be.

The way things were now. She saw the deep, profound connection she shared with Uraza — manifested in threads of light that tethered mankind to the kingdom of beasts — that they all shared with their spirit animals and with every living thing.

She saw death . . . and she saw rebirth.

Somehow, Abeke *understood* it. She understood all of it. She tasted salt on her lips, and she no longer questioned whether or not the water running down her face was rain or something more.

This is the end, Abeke thought. She looked to Conor, who knelt over Briggan, his tears flowing freely, and the realization finally hit her that this was the moment when she might lose Uraza. The thought made her gasp in pain. She turned back to her leopard, who met her gaze with steady violet eyes. Then she wrapped her arms around Uraza's neck and hugged her tight. The memory flooded back to her of when she'd drank the Nectar of Ninani so long ago, and how she'd felt when she first saw the sleek golden leopard. How much they had experienced together since then. How much they had won and lost. What would life be like without her?

"Thank you," Abeke whispered into Uraza's fur.

Uraza didn't respond. Instead, she stayed calm and still. Abeke could feel the tremor of her purr, as if her spirit animal was telling her that everything would be all right.

Abeke closed her eyes and waited for the end.

22

REBIRTH

CONOR DIDN'T KNOW HOW IT WOULD HAPPEN. WOULD Briggan disappear in a flash of light, just like the others had? Would the dying Evertree reclaim him, somehow? Or would he simply die, the way Conor had seen sheep die before, the way so many who'd crossed their paths had already died? Conor ran his hand absently through Briggan's fur. He bowed his head and braced himself. He'd always sympathized with those who lost their spirit animals, and he'd told himself to be ready for this moment ever since he first felt it during his visions.

But I'm not ready. He could never be ready. And now, the time had come.

The visions continued to shift in color. Through them, Conor saw each of the Great Beasts as they once were—Tellun, Rumfuss, Arax, then Kovo, Gerathon, and Halawir, then the others, all settling into the far reaches of the world. They vanished from sight, leaving behind bright balls of energy that swirled around the image of the once mighty Evertree. Conor saw a vision of Uraza appear in all her glory, a full-sized Great Beast. She appeared to walk toward them, and as they looked on, she turned her violet eyes toward where Abeke and the real Uraza sat.

A vision of Jhi soon joined her, as large and magnificent as she once was. Mighty Essix soared down toward them. And Briggan . . . an image of Briggan as a Great Beast appeared in the sky last, the elegant and towering shape of a beautiful wolf, loping easily up to the others and stopping at their side. The vision of Briggan looked down at Conor, then at the wounded version of himself that lay on the grass. The vision gave a single nod.

Then, all the colors in the sky faded away. The clouds returned to normal, and sheets of rain continued to pour down.

He looked down at Briggan, who gazed up at him with a bemused expression. *Our spirit animals will not die*, Conor suddenly realized. The wolf pushed himself up to a sitting position, still wounded, but otherwise alive. "You're going to be okay, aren't you?" Conor said hoarsely to Briggan.

Briggan nodded, just like his vision had.

Stunned, Abeke looked back and forth between Conor and Briggan. "But—I thought you said . . ." she began, "that our spirit animals didn't live through this journey. I thought the other Great Beasts all sacrificed themselves. Uraza—"

"—had already given her life once." Conor finished the sentence, finally understanding what the vision in the sky had meant. He broke into a huge smile as he faced the others. "The Four Fallen won't need to sacrifice themselves again."

Silence.

Until Rollan broke it with a huge whoop. He flung himself around Essix's neck, to her startlement, and hugged her tight. They all broke into cheers. Conor threw his arms around Briggan's neck. He couldn't tell if he was laughing or crying, but it didn't matter. Relief flooded him. Briggan was alive! So were the other Four Fallen. Even through his grief at the Evertree's death and the sacrifices of the other Great Beasts, at least his spirit animal was going to be okay. They had defeated Kovo. That was what really mattered.

"Hey—there he goes!"

Meilin's voice shook Conor out of his moment. He glanced over to where Meilin was pointing to a figure fleeing from them. Shane had taken advantage of their celebration in order to sneak away.

"That little coward—" Rollan growled, picking himself up and getting ready to chase after him.

Abeke was the one who grabbed his arm and held him back. She shook her head. "Let him go," she said.

"Really?" Rollan exclaimed. "After all that!"

"We're no better if we have no mercy," Abeke replied, watching Shane's back as he ran, stumbling, away from them. She took a deep breath. "He won't bother us again." Conor knew she was remembering the moment during their battle when Shane had thrown himself at Kovo in an attempt to buy them some time. All of his anger at the former Devourer seemed to diffuse.

So they stayed where they were, looking on until Shane became nothing more than a dot on the rainy horizon.

"Now what?" Meilin asked as Conor finally pushed

himself up onto his feet. She stared sadly at the fallen Evertree. "The Great Beasts are gone."

Conor's attention shifted to the Staff of Cycles. It still lay in the grass near the Evertree, right where he had dropped it. He walked over to the staff, Briggan limping at his side. Conor reached it, picked it up gingerly, and studied it. The staff no longer looked as silver and glittering as it once had. In fact, it looked like any ordinary spiral of wood, even like his shepherd's crook. Only small hints of luster still glinted along the shaft. Otherwise, it had turned wholly unremarkable.

Conor stared at the fallen Evertree. He walked over to it, where the golden color of its leaves had already begun to fade. He bowed his head in reverence before the twisted trunk and branches, then put the Staff of Cycles gently down in the dirt where its roots emerged from the ground.

"I'm sorry," he said. Tears sprang to his eyes.

A ripple seemed to go through the earth, but Conor ignored it, thinking it was just the wind and rain beating against him.

Then he felt the pulse again. It was like a wave had moved through the ground beneath him, the heartbeat of something *living*. Of the land itself.

He frowned, looking around. His eyes settled on the Staff of Cycles—which once more had started to glow a faint silver color.

Gradually the glow traveled to the Evertree, spreading along the length of its branches and trunk until it engulfed the entire mass of broken wood. The glow left the Evertree, then pooled into the ground around it. As everyone looked on, the torn earth from where the Evertree's roots had ripped out now began to part. A bright light emerged from somewhere deep in the soil, revealing something small, new, and green.

A seedling!

It was nothing more than a slender stalk of a plant, still curved in infanthood and emerging from a split seed, its two delicate leaves tipped with silver and gold. The first hints of roots extended from the seed's cracks, reaching toward the ground, growing thicker and stronger with each passing moment. Conor sat down beside Briggan and watched in awe.

A new beginning. *A new Evertree.*

Conor had a feeling that, someday, when the Evertree became whole again, the other Great Beasts might return once more to Erdas. The cycle would begin anew. His arm tightened around Briggan's neck, and calmness filled his heart. Someday, Briggan might evolve back into his Great Beast form. Conor didn't know if he would be around to see it, but . . . that was okay. Everything would begin again.

REUNION

THE RAIN DIDN'T LAST LONG.

Soon the clouds began to clear, revealing first a pocket of gray light, the hints of dawn, and then the brilliant gold and faint blue of a beautiful morning. Water beaded on the grasses of the crater, turning into a million sparkling gems under the light. The breeze brought with it the first true scent of summer, something sweet and fresh, nothing like the oppressive air that had seemed to hover over them for the past few weeks.

It felt as if a spell had lifted from all of Erdas.

Rollan smiled as they made their way down from the crater and out toward Nilo's southern shores. Essix soared above them, while Uraza loped ahead toward the water. Briggan and Jhi stayed with Conor and Meilin. The sun felt warm on Rollan's face, and at the sight of the blue ocean, a wild joy built up in his chest. He broke into a run. The others followed behind him, cheering and laughing. Rollan blushed when he saw Meilin sprinting beside him, an enormous smile on her face. She flashed a grin at him, and his own smile grew wider.

They all slowed to a stop as they reached the shore. The waves crashed in perfect arcs, sliding white foam up the sand and toward their feet. Rollan pulled off his boots and let his toes wriggle in the surf. He breathed deeply. The air was salty and cool. Nearby, Uraza leaned her head forward and tentatively sniffed at the water. Behind her, Jhi ambled up. The panda paused behind Uraza, rolled her silver eyes innocently skyward, and gave the great cat a playful nudge. Uraza fell forward into the surf. She immediately pounced up, shaking water from her head, and gave Jhi a grumpy swat with her paw. Jhi just blinked big, sweet eyes back.

Abeke and Meilin laughed as Uraza chased Jhi along the shore, the two acting for a moment like they were young cubs.

"I wonder if Olvan's forces defeated the Conquerors," Conor said as they all joined Rollan.

"Maybe they're already sailing for Greenhaven," Meilin added.

Rollan smiled at that thought. He pictured the gray mood lifted from Greenhaven, and how beautiful the hills must be now. He looked down the line of Nilo's coast that curved off into the horizon. "It will be a long journey back," he said.

Abeke nodded, but she had a smile on her face too. "A journey spent in the best company." She looked at Meilin as she said it, and Meilin beamed.

"One more journey," Meilin replied. "A victory march."

Rollan nudged Meilin in the ribs with his elbow. He gave her a sidelong grin. "I bet I can beat you back to Greenhaven."

Meilin raised an amused eyebrow. "Is that so?"

"Hey, you've been gone for a long while, and I've been training. Just saying."

Meilin merely grinned. "Then let's see a demonstration."

Rollan tossed hair out of his face. Then, without warning, he darted down the shore.

"Hey!" Meilin exclaimed. "No warning? No 'on your mark'?" She bolted too, leaving Abeke and Conor to jog along behind them, grinning at their antics.

Some things would never change. Meilin caught up to Rollan and passed him. As she did, he caught her, threw an arm around her neck, and ruffled up her hair. Meilin squealed, her laughter ringing out in the clean ocean air.

It was so nice to laugh.

It was so nice to head home.

* * *

The storms stopped in Zhong, and the earthquakes quieted in Eura. The snow disappeared from Nilo, unveiling the land in its former beauty.

Even better, the Conquerors had been defeated. With Gerathon's death, the Bile had lost its power over those who drank it. In that instant, nearly half of the Conqueror armies had simply abandoned the battle. The rest quickly surrendered.

As they sailed back toward Greenhaven, the four saw all the signs of normalcy returning to the world. Relieved looks graced the people's faces in port cities. Clusters of cheering citizens sometimes gathered on the shores to watch the Greencloaks sail by.

Still, signs of healing did not mean that tragedy was forgotten. The land bridge between Stetriol and Nilo remained, and many cities were still picking up the pieces, building new homes and farms around broken, collapsed ones. Erdas would take time to heal. Without the Nectar of Ninani, no one could be sure how the future would look for new bonds with spirit animals, or even that bonds could happen at all, until the new Evertree matured. But one thing was for sure: The bonding sickness was gone, and with it, the Bile and the Nectar.

The links between man and animal could begin anew.

On a beautiful, warm afternoon, the Four Fallen and the Greencloaks' caravan finally docked at home. As they made the final leg of their journey, Rollan could see the spires and battlements of Greenhaven Castle peeking out from the climb from the docks, basking under the light of a bright sun.

Overhead, Essix soared and let out a call of fierce joy. Rollan smiled as he looked up at her tiny figure, then turned back to the castle's silhouette.

"I can't believe you actually became a Greencloak," Meilin said as she walked beside him. She shot him a quick smile.

"Me neither," Rollan replied. "I look awful in green." Even as he smiled back, the memory of Tarik came fresh to him, bringing with it a sharp stab of pain. Rollan imagined Tarik was still alive, traveling home with them now. What would he have made of everything they'd accomplished?

Meilin watched him thoughtfully, as if she knew what he was thinking.

"Do you think Tarik would have been proud of me?" Rollan asked in a soft voice.

Meilin reached over to take his hand. She squeezed it once. "I know he would be," she replied.

"Hey, guys," Conor said as he trotted back to them. Abeke walked nearby too, unable to contain her excitement. "Look at the crowd that's gathered near the castle. They're all waiting for us!"

Rollan craned his neck. Conor was right; as they crested the top of the staircase, he saw before the castle's silhouette a mass of people, their faint chants carried on the wind. Rollan thought they were chanting something about victory and the Four Fallen. He certainly recognized a cheer for Essix.

"Let's go join the party, then," Rollan exclaimed, hurrying upward.

It seemed like the closer they came, the bigger the crowd got. By the time they crested the final staircase and saw the sprawling courtyard of Greenhaven Castle, masses of people had completely filled either side.

"The Four Fallen have returned!" someone yelled as they approached. "The heroes are back!"

The cheers were deafening. Rollan waved enthusiastically as their procession passed through the crowds, while Conor bowed his head in humble acknowledgment. Abeke and Meilin just gaped in awe. With the people were also spirit animals — a beautiful crested heron next to a girl with pigtails, a boy with a white-faced monkey sitting on his shoulder, another boy with a hedgehog. As they threw rice and colorful strips of paper in the air, the heron flapped its wings to blow the paper toward them. Rollan laughed, swatting the strips away.

"Mom!"

Conor's shout stopped Rollan short. His eyes darted to where Conor was looking, and there, he saw Conor's mother and family rushing out of the packed crowds and onto the courtyard's center. Conor pushed forward, stumbling in his haste, and then ran toward her. She pulled him into a huge hug.

Abeke let out a startled laugh from where she walked Her father and sister waved at her from the side of the street. They had come to see her! Rollan couldn't stop smiling as, in spite of everything, she rushed over to them. She paused for a moment right as she reached them, as if unsure what to do next, but Soama pulled her into a hug, and Pojalo put his hands on their shoulders.

Rollan searched in vain for a sign of his own mother. *I won't find her here*, he reminded himself with a sinking heart. Gerathon was gone now, and though his mother no longer needed to obey the Bile or live in fear – she had been with the Conquerors. Meilin and Abeke had both seen her in Nilo. Even with the Conquerors dissolving after their losses, there would be no reason for her to come *here*.

What wishful thinking. Rollan steeled his heart. *Expectations just lead to disappointment*, he reminded himself. He looked back at Conor hugging his family and tried to imagine himself in the same place, tried to convince himself that seeing his friend's joy would be the same as experiencing his own.

"Rollan?"

The voice was quiet, so quiet that Rollan barely heard it. He whirled back around. Where did it come from? He looked at the cheering faces, but saw no one familiar looking back. A sinking feeling settled in his chest. Perhaps he'd imagined the voice. Rollan shook his head and was about to turn away when he heard it again.

"Rollan! Rollan!"

"Look!" Meilin exclaimed, pointing into the crowd. There Rollan saw a frantically waving hand making its way closer through the people. It was a woman. She had dark hair and tanned skin, and her eyes were a warm, breathtaking brown. He watched her as she made her way into the street, but even when she stood there, right before him, he could hardly believe the sight.

Mother?

She didn't look like she had the last time he'd seen her. She looked happy now. Free.

Rollan couldn't remember stepping forward. He couldn't remember if he said anything, if he called out for her like Conor had, or even if he bothered to smile or laugh or cry. All he remembered was running across the cobblestones. One moment he was still with the rest of the procession, and the next, he was in his mother's arms, holding on for dear life. He was laughing. Crying? He didn't care.

"You're here!" he said.

Aidana didn't answer. Maybe there wasn't much that needed to be said, at least not yet. So she hugged him tight, and he returned the embrace. How long ago had it been since Rollan sat in a filthy dungeon cell, a lost orphan that nobody wanted? How much had changed. He smiled so hard that it hurt.

Through a haze of joy, Rollan realized that Abeke had stepped over to join him in his celebration, along with her father and sister. Conor and his family were hurrying up the path toward them. Rollan wiped his eyes and laughed. Then he gazed at where Meilin still stood, alone.

She was smiling too, but in the midst of all these family reunions, she looked a little lost, as if unsure whether or not she should be allowed to join them. Rollan's smile wavered for a moment.

Meilin's father was gone. She would have no reunion here today. When she saw Rollan's face, she smiled wider in an attempt to hide her sadness.

"Meilin," Rollan called out. He motioned for her to come over.

She hesitated, but when Abeke and Conor piped up too, Meilin took a tentative step forward, and then headed over with a shy smile. "Hi," she said softly to their gathered families.

Aidana smiled warmly at her, then patted her cheek. "Hello, my darling," she replied. And before Meilin could utter anything else, Rollan's mother pulled her into a tight hug.

They all joined in, Abeke, Conor, and Rollan, until they were one big pile of arms and legs and hearts and smiles. Rollan found Meilin and wrapped his arm around her shoulders. He looked from her to Conor, then to Abeke. "We'll always have a family," he said. *"Always."*

At those words, Meilin's moment of sadness faded away, and her smile turned genuine. She hugged them all back.

If Rollan used Essix's vision right then, he would see, among the throngs of celebrating revelers, a tiny, almost insignificant cluster of friends wearing cloaks of green, each blending in with the ones next to it, so that no one could tell where one ended and the others began.

They were one.

The End

You've read the book — now join the adventure at **Scholastic.com/SpiritAnimals**!

Enter the world of Erdas, where YOU are one of the rare few to summon a spirit animal.

Create your character.

Choose your spirit animal.

THE LEGEND LIVES IN YOU